EVERYTHING I'M NOT

SARA MULLINS

For my loving husband, David, and sons, Carter and Levi. Your love and support mean the world to me.

I would also like to dedicate this to those we've lost to Covid-19 and their loving families.

ACKNOWLEDGMENTS

Many thanks to my husband, David, and children for your patience and encouragement. This journey is special to me because I get to share it with all of you.

To my sister, Carey. Thank you for being my first reader and providing your feedback. I appreciate your help and honesty.

To The Next Chapter Publishing team for your support. I am grateful for the opportunity you have given me.

CHAPTER 1

The four tiny feet of one plump rat scurried across a pair of flannel pants. The woman wearing them was lying on a slab of concrete. Her eyelids twitched as the tickling sensation started to wake her. She slowly opened her eye, just enough to let in some hazy light. Her irises rolled back and forth for a moment. She clenched her eyelids tight, then lifted her head off the floor, and opened her eyes fully.

As she regained consciousness, the reality of her environment began to set in. The tape over her mouth restricted her accelerated breathing. Her eyes finally began to focus. She looked down at the rat, which had paused in its journey, and her throat attempted a shriek at the sight. Her ankles had been taped, but she did the best she could to kick her legs. Both of her arms were bound together behind her back. She struggled to maneuver, gradually pulling her body up into a sitting position.

The woman took several deep breaths through her nose as she looked around the room. Cold tears rolled down her quivering cheeks. She couldn't make out many details. Only one beam of light shined in from a miniature window near the ceiling. There didn't seem to be much in the room besides some shelves on the nearest wall, and a broken chair discarded in the corner. An awful, musty smell lingered in the air. Other than the scratching of rodents and the distant trickling of water, the room was scarily quiet.

She sat alone in the dark, thinking, problem-solving. The only thing she could contemplate doing was to make her way to the shelves to try to find something, anything, that could help her situation. She used her heels and buttocks to scoot across the dusty floor until she approached the old wooden ledges. There wasn't much on the bottom one, other than an old pair of shoes and a cardboard box. Both looked as if they had been there for a decade. The next shelf up was a little more promising. Four Mason jars sat in a row. They, too, appeared like they had been there for many years. She raised her brows, hopeful that a broken jar could help with the tape. If she could just knock one down.

The quiet was suddenly interrupted. Footsteps creaked on the wooden boards above her head. Clouds of dust drifted down with every step. The woman stopped moving, her heart rate doubled, and her breaths trembled. She listened as quietly as possible while the sound of the steps made its way across the room to the other side. It grew quiet again, only for a moment, then she heard keys. A padlock jostled on a door she couldn't see. Another tear rolled down her face as she waited for the door to open.

Reagan gasped and sat up quickly on the sofa in her living room. Her heart was pounding hard enough to feel it in her throat. She took a deep breath and raised a hand to her chest, grateful that she was in her home. She looked at her watch and shook her head. *When did I fall asleep?* The complaints of a teenage girl filtered through from across the house. Reagan stood up and made her way down the hall. She approached the doorway of the unhappy adolescent with caution.

One by one, the shirts that comprised Emma's wardrobe were being removed from the closet and returned with fury. She yanked another hanger off the rod and held the blouse up to her chest, looking in the mirror. Finally satisfied with what she saw, she slipped the shirt on and examined every possible angle in the mirror.

"Where are you going?" her mother asked from the doorway.

"Out," Emma grumbled, not removing her gaze from the mirror. She grabbed a pair of shoes from the closet and slipped them onto her feet. Her mother's burning stare practically forced her to look up. "What?"

Reagan tried to remain serious, but she suspected the worry consuming her began to show on her face none the less. "I just . . ."

"Mom, I don't get you. What is your problem with Evan? I like him. He likes me. Are you going to question me every time I want to see him?"

"No, it's just . . . I worry about you, that's all," Reagan replied.

"Why, because he's eighteen?"

"That, and you're sixteen, Emma. He just graduated. He'll be going to college soon."

"I know, mom. Is that all?" Emma snapped.

"Well, to be honest with you, I don't like the way he talks to you. He's a little arrogant and controlling."

Emma shook her head and looked up at the ceiling. "He cares about me! You are unbelievable. You think you know everyth-"

"Stop it, Emma! That's enough. You don't talk to your mother that way. I'm sorry for questioning you, but I'm only doing it because I care about you. I don't want you to get hurt," Reagan said, dropping her head.

Emma rolled her eyes then looked back to her mom. They both remained silent, digesting each other's words until Reagan could think of what to say next. Emma began picking at her nails, as if waiting for the next lecture.

"Have I ever told you how your dad and I met?" Reagan asked.

"You met at the mall, right?"

"Yes, but there's more to it than that. I was a very quiet girl. I didn't have many friends or much confidence in myself. Then I met your dad and, at first, I didn't think that he could like, let alone love, someone like me. But after what he did for me, I knew in my heart that he loved me."

"What did he do?" Emma asked.

"Well, I can tell you, but only if you have time to sit and talk with your mom."

Emma looked down at her shoes and grinned, before gazing back up. "I guess we can talk for a little bit. I mean, I really don't need to leave until six anyway."

"Why were you getting ready so early?" Reagan asked.

"I don't know. I'm bored I guess," Emma replied.

Her mom chuckled and walked over to her daughter. "Well, come sit with me. I should just start from the beginning."

CHAPTER 2

The Greenbriar Mall was the only one of its kind in Newbrook, Ohio, and about the only place in town where Reagan could work at that time. She hadn't yet utilized her college education and had zero desire to flip burgers. Since receiving her degrees in art and business, she had spent two years trying to formulate a plan of what to do with them. Now she was starting to question why she had picked those majors in the first place. After all, art is a tough career to pursue.

Reagan wasn't the only one struggling, though. The last decade had brought a steady economic decline to the small mid-western town, and its faithful citizens were starting to feel the impact. Reagan considered herself lucky to have a job at all. She had an apartment and a car, neither of which were in prime condition, but they fulfilled the requirements.

On this morning in December, the chill outside had frosted up her windshield. At first, she waited patiently in her driver's seat for the car to warm up. But eventually, she gave in to the urge to use her windshield solution and wipers to speed up the process. Although she didn't much like going to work, she liked the drive this time of year. The town that could seem so drab at times, found a way to look beautiful when decorated with

Christmas lights. It almost had her convinced that things were going to get better.

Her life had been fairly uneventful up to that point. She was an only child, and a quiet one to boot. Her parents were always supportive, and quite invisible to the rest of the town. They lived the typical middle-class life – no mansion and no extravagant pool, but they had running cars, a roof over their heads, and food on the table. Reagan graduated high school with the third-highest GPA in her class and a couple of friendships that were sure to last a lifetime. Her senior prom was a girl's night out for her and two friends. It was fun, but maybe not what one thinks of when they envision the prom.

She was living two hours away from her childhood home now, attempting to live the life of the independent child who has left the nest and started a glamorous life of their own. The truth, though, was that Reagan was still waiting on the glamor. Lost, lonely, and on the verge of moving back home, she was losing her ambition to follow the dream that had left her in debt.

Reagan walked into the mall and made her way to Katie's, the small clothing store that provided her paycheck every other week. She worked with the same group of girls Monday through Friday, but only Jen ever seemed to notice her. The others were usually consumed by thoughts of their makeup or what episode was coming on that night. Needless to say, Reagan was anything but surprised when she strolled into the store and saw Beth, Tina, and Valerie gossiping about the latest town break-up. They all glanced at Reagan when she walked by, then returned to their conversation with synchronized smirks.

Jen was already in the break room, attempting to stuff her coat into her locker. She tucked the sleeve in three times, then tried to shut the door.

"Oh . . . my . . . God. What a piece of shit!" Jen shouted at the metal door. She lifted her head at the sight of Reagan's shadow. "Damn, you scared the crap out of me," Jen said, clutching her chest.

"Sorry, I didn't mean to," Reagan said softly.

"It's okay. Aren't you excited for another day in this hell hole?"

Reagan let out a chuckle. "Yeah, I can't wait."

"What are the girls talking about this time? I can hear them from here."

"I don't know for sure, but it sounded like another break-up."

"Oh God, give me a break. How many people can they possibly know in this town?" Jen said.

"A lot more than me, I guess."

"That's okay, you're better off. Most people are assholes."

Reagan grinned and opened her locker. She was used to Jen's pessimism, perhaps realism. Whatever it was, Jen had developed a sort of "kiss my ass" attitude toward the world. Supposedly, she had been a completely different person as a teenager. According to Jen, she was shy and obedient, a far cry from the rough and tough new version of herself that Reagan knew. Reagan just assumed she got tired of trying to be perfect all the time.

The two of them meandered out to the floor to get ready for the day. The other girls had begun folding clothes and straightening up. Reagan made her way to one cash register and Jen stood at the other. The manager, Angie, usually arranged them like this. It was the perfect setup for utilizing their strengths. Of course, they were all content with the organization. Angie, while only being a few years older than the rest of them, was well experienced. She had started working there in high school and stuck around longer than the average employee.

A few hours into her shift, Reagan checked in with Jen to make sure she would be all right on her own for a few minutes. She walked back to the break room and collapsed into one of the chairs at the table. Her feet were grateful for the time off. For some reason, the store was exceptionally slow, considering the time of year. This seemed like the perfect opportunity to relax and have a quick bite to eat.

Of course, her moment of peace was short-lived, since Tina decided to take her break at the same time. Reagan looked up from her sandwich when she walked in the door, making uncomfortable eye contact. Tina quickly lifted her nose and made her way to the refrigerator. Reagan continued to eat and read her magazine in silence, until the shrieking sound of Tina's phone filled the room. Reagan jumped a little in her seat at the sudden noise.

"Hello?" Tina answered. "I'm at work, Derek, I told you that." She started giggling and twirled her hair. "Yeah, we'll see about that later." She laughed again and looked over at Reagan, who had glanced up for just a moment. "I can't talk right now, I'll call you later . . . yeah, I hear you . . . okay, I hear you . . . see you tonight."

Tina shook her head and shut the refrigerator door before turning to face Reagan. She felt Tina's eyes on her but continued to read her magazine anyway.

"That's called a boyfriend, Reagan. Maybe you should try to get one, instead of reading about it all the time," Tina said.

"I really don't care what you think," Reagan replied.

"Whatever, you're so weird." Tina rolled her eyes and walked out with her water.

A few minutes later, Reagan decided to walk back out to take over for Jen. She ignored the other girls on her way through the store and stepped back up to her cash register. "Was it busy?" she asked.

"No, not really."

"I got this, if you wanna go now."

"Thanks, girl. I'll be right back," Jen said.

"Take your time."

Jen disappeared into the back and, just as she had said, there were hardly any customers in the store. One woman stood in the men's section with her little girl, scanning for the right size pants. A couple of high school girls looked at the sweaters, leaving them unfolded when they were finished. Beth and Valerie stood off to the side, shaking their heads in disgust, knowing they would have to refold them.

Reagan stared out the front door at the bookstore across the hallway. She was envious of the patrons within. For them, it was acceptable to drink coffee and read a good story. A couple of children sat on the floor and flipped through the pages of a pop-up book, while their mother examined the romance section. Reagan had disappeared into a daydream, but it didn't last long.

A trio of guys suddenly blocked her view of the bookstore, as they strolled through the doorway. The first two were walking side-by-side, still laughing about something that had happened in the hallway. Both were dressed well and walked confidently. They were hard to tell apart, other than the color of their shirts. The third man followed up the rear, smiling at the humorous actions of the other two. He was the tallest of the group and sported a simple t-shirt and pair of jeans. His hair was dark and messy, and his eyes were the color of milk chocolate. He strolled into the store without a care in the world, hands in his pockets.

Reagan watched him as the group meandered toward the men's clothes. Something about him drew her gaze. He was nothing like the type of guys she tended to get along with. Normally, the popular ones regarded her as invisible, and she settled for that, as long as she wasn't a laughingstock. She had tried to avoid the cool kids her whole childhood and she had carried this attitude into her adult life. Not only did they often treat her like dirt, but she also believed it was a waste of her time to try to have a conversation with them. This assumption was a safety net for her, and it tended to pay off.

The guy she was watching wandered away from the other two for a moment. To her surprise, his demeanor seemed to change a little when he stood alone. He reached for the green shirt hanging on the rack in front of him and looked it over. After apparently deciding against it, he put it back, then paused for a moment. Her burning gaze must have begun to get his attention. He turned and looked over his shoulder, to find Reagan's eyes all over him. She immediately felt her cheeks heating, and she looked at the register, hoping to play it off. He watched her for a moment, but that was all he would get. Valerie had seen him from across the room and decided to do what she did best . . . flirt.

"Hey, Jackson," her squeaky voice called out. "I haven't seen you in here before."

"Well, that's probably 'cause I usually don't shop here. We were just walkin' around, wastin' time. They walked in and I followed." He looked down at her for just a second, then back at the rack.

Valerie giggled. "So how have you been? What's it been, like, five years?"

He gave her what appeared to be a forced smile. "Yeah, somethin' like that."

His disinterest was escaping her attention, so she continued.

"Can I help you find something?"

Reagan watched from the cash register and rolled her eyes at Valerie's pathetic display. She had seen the girls in action before, but it was equally ridiculous every time it happened.

"I'm fine, really. Thanks, though, uh . . ." he hesitated.

"Valerie, remember?"

"Yeah, that's right. Sorry, I have a terrible memory sometimes."

Reagan chuckled out loud, then cleared her throat and looked down at the fliers on the counter, hoping to remain unnoticed. Jen walked up behind her just in time.

"What ya laughin' at?"

"Nothing. Just the same ol' Valerie," Reagan answered.

Jen looked over at Valerie, who was desperately trying to get in one more question. "How pathetic. She thinks that all men will bow down to her, doesn't she?"

"Seems that way."

Reagan chatted with Jen and found busy-work to do, but she kept glancing back at Jackson. Valerie had walked away and was now talking to the girls on the other end of the store. Reagan could only imagine the exaggerated story she was telling them about the good-looking guy from high school.

Jackson had finally picked out a shirt and was waiting patiently on his friends to finish browsing. He leaned against the wall, but at least one part of his body was always on the move. His restlessness got the best of him and he began pacing. He started toward the winter gear, then noticed Valerie watching him again. A look of panic struck him, and he performed an about-face. Then he did something that Reagan did not expect; he looked right at her. She forced herself to look back at him, in the most awkward way possible. Her top and bottom teeth pinched her bottom lip. He walked up to her cash register and laid the shirt down.

"Is this everything?" she asked him.

"Yeah, this is it."

Reagan scanned the tag. "That'll be twenty-one eighty-seven, please." She folded the shirt and stuck it in a bag, while he swiped his card. "You want the receipt in the bag?"

"Sure, that's fine."

He looked over at his friends. They were still checking out the same sweatshirts as five minutes earlier.

"Thank you," Reagan said, handing him the bag.

"So, have you worked here for a while?" he asked quietly.

"Me?"

He grinned. "Yeah."

"A little more than a year I guess," she replied.

Jen inconspicuously watched out of the corner of her eye.

"That's cool. What's your n . . ." he started, only to be interrupted by his friends.

"Jackson, are you ready?" the guy in blue asked.

"Am I ready? You guys stood there for, like, fifteen minutes and you're not getting anything?" Jackson asked.

"Nah, I didn't like anything."

Jackson laughed. "Alright, man, we're going." He looked back at Reagan for a moment.

His friends noticed his gaze. They glanced in her direction, then back at him. One smirked and the other awkwardly tried not to laugh.

"Dude, let's go," said his buddy in gray.

"Alright, damn," Jackson replied. He gave her one last look, then followed his friends out the door.

Jen waited until the coast was clear before turning toward Reagan. "And who was that?" she asked her.

"I have no idea."

"He seemed interested in you."

"No. No one is *ever* interested in me," Reagan said, shaking her head.

"I really think he was. His friends just blew it for him, that's all."

Reagan laughed. "Jen, trust me. Guys don't notice me. They never have. I'm just, well, I'm plain."

"Hey, you're not plain. You're real. Just because you're not always putting on a show for guys, doesn't mean you're plain. The good guys, the ones worth getting, will see that. They don't want fake girls," Jen encouraged.

"You think so?"

"Oh yeah. Ask anyone. Except for them, of course," she said, pointing at the girls.

Reagan chuckled and looked at her shoes. "Valerie tried talking to him, but he kind of blew her off. It was hilarious."

"Ya see? That's what I'm talking about."

"All right, I believe you. Either way, I have no clue who he is, other than the fact that she said his name. So that means that the one and only guy that may have been interested in me is gone and I don't know who he is. That's great," she said.

"He knows where you are, though," Jen replied.

Reagan nodded and they went back to work.

On her way home, the sky grew dark, and the temperature held at a brisk twenty-six degrees, as it had done all day. Flurries had already started falling at the beginning of what was expected to be a significant snowfall. Of course, what folks in Newbrook considered to be a significant snowfall was at least six inches, otherwise it wasn't worth worrying about. Reagan had no issues with the anticipated blanket of precipitation. The snow was soothing for her. There was a peace associated with it that she couldn't compare to anything else. Perhaps it was because of the fun she'd had sledding as a child, or the snow days where she didn't have to endure the pain of school. Either way, at twenty-four years old, she was still comforted by it.

When she got home, she rummaged through the cabinet, trying to figure out what she should eat for dinner. A can of chicken noodle soup was decidedly the perfect choice for the weather. She curled up on the couch with her soup and the newest book that she had just started that Monday. The thought of her day at work, and her brief interaction with Jackson, crossed her mind. She looked at the book in her hand and wondered if most women her age were living a more exhilarating life. Then Reagan remembered what Jen had said to her and it brought her hope. Hearing such a thing from someone other than her parents was indeed a confidence booster.

CHAPTER 3

The next day, Reagan decided to visit the library. She had completed the romance book she was reading the night before. The woman that worked at the counter anticipated her arrival every Saturday morning. At this point, she was practically on her way to getting a key for the front door.

"Good morning, Reagan," the woman said.

"Morning, Donna."

"So . . . was it good?" Donna asked.

Reagan smiled and strolled up to the counter. "It was so good. I couldn't believe the way he proposed to her."

"I know, I cried. Isn't that pathetic?"

"No, don't feel bad. I cry all the time when I read romance." Reagan chuckled and slid the book to Donna.

"You know, Mary is talking about retiring soon. You should apply here once she leaves," Donna said.

"You think so?"

"Oh yeah, this would be the perfect job for you. Heck, you're here more than I am sometimes."

"Come on now, that's not true." Reagan paused for a second as Donna raised her right eyebrow. "Okay, it's kind of true, but do you blame me? I live alone, I have a job that I don't like, and two degrees that I'm not using. I have no clue what I'm doing or what I'm going to do. So, I fill in the void with books and movies. And that's the extent of my lonely life."

"Wow, that's deep, sweetie. Sorry, I wasn't trying to bother you. I thought you'd like to know, in case you were at least interested in changing your job," Donna said.

"No, you're right. It would be a good start at making a change. Let me know when she decides to retire, and I'll apply," Reagan replied.

"Will do."

Reagan found herself a new book to read and stopped again to see Donna, before heading out the door. She handed over her library card and waited on Donna to do her thing.

"Here you go, honey. Enjoy," Donna said.

"I'm sure I will," Reagan replied.

"See you next Saturday," Donna added.

Reagan nodded. "See ya."

She turned and walked back out the door, reading the back of the book. She didn't pay much attention to the world around her as she strolled down the sidewalk. This Saturday morning routine had become an essential part of her life. Luckily, her apartment was only a few blocks away from the library, making for the perfect opportunity to get exercise. She wrapped her scarf around one more time in attempt to seal out the cold air. For the most part, the small town was peaceful this time of day. The crunching sound of the salt beneath her boots was only interrupted by the occasional passing car.

She flipped to the inside of the novel and began reading it as she walked along. Then her salt-crushing commotion was joined by the sound of another pair of boots. Reagan immediately grew uncomfortable. Her loner lifestyle created a certain amount of awkwardness when she was approached by other human beings. She didn't know whether to slow down or speed up, so she decided to focus on the pages and truck forward.

"Uh, hello?" a man's voice said from behind her.

She stopped and whipped around, prepared to grab the pepper spray from her purse if needed. Reagan looked up at the pair of eyes staring back at her. She hadn't forgotten the chocolate brown irises that peered down at her.

"Hi," she said, almost as if it was a question.

"I'm sorry, I wasn't trying to scare you. I saw you walk out of the library and I thought . . ." he trailed off. She gazed up at him. Was he waiting on her to say something? Then he continued, "You work at the mall, right?"

"Yes," she replied without another word.

"I thought it was you," he said. She looked down at her twiddling thumbs within the blue gloves that covered them. He seemed to sense her uneasiness. "It's okay, I really am sorry. I shouldn't have walked up behind you like that. I just wanted to make sure I got the chance to say something this time." He held out his hand. "I'm Jackson."

She grinned a little and shifted the book to her left hand before reaching with her right. "Reagan."

"Reagan? I like that," he said.

"Thanks."

"It's different. You don't hear it a lot."

"Well, different is sort of my middle name," she said, chuckling.

"That's okay. That's good, actually. I admire people that are unique."

"You do?"

"Yeah. It's so easy to try to be like everyone else. But to be different than the crowd . . . well, that takes courage sometimes."

Reagan blushed and looked down at her black boots. She didn't know what to say next. She not only spent very little time talking to other people, but also only had a minuscule amount of experience with guys. All the romance books she had checked out hadn't quite prepared her for a face-to-face moment with a man. And a handsome man he was.

"I better get going," she said. These weren't the words that she truly wanted to spew out of her mouth, but she was too scared to say anything else.

"Okay. Um, do you want me to walk you home or anything?" he offered.

"No, that's okay. I only have a few blocks to go. Thank you, though."

"You're welcome. I'll see ya around."

"See ya." She turned and started to walk away, scrunching her face in disgust with herself. *What is wrong with you, Reagan? Just let him walk with you. Why do you have to be so weird?*

She continued down the sidewalk, questioning her decision-making skills. Jackson grinned and stuffed his hands into his pockets. He glanced at her one last time, then turned back toward his car, parked at the hardware store across from the library.

Monday morning saw Reagan heading to work again for another day of Christmas shoppers. The thought of going to the mall was nauseating. Jen was about the only part of the experience that she could stand. The job at the library was becoming more enticing by the hour. All she could do was wait on the news from Donna and keep chugging along to get a paycheck. Her goal was to save as much as she could, hoping to one day live out her dream. She had chosen to study the subjects she picked because she cherished the idea of opening a store to sell her artwork. Getting to that point, without losing her mind first, was starting to become a challenge.

"Another glorious day," Jen said to Reagan as they stuffed their coats into their lockers.

"I hate it," Reagan replied instinctively.

"Me too. But look at the bright side. You at least have a shot at having a future. You were smart and went to college. I have nothing and I'll be stuck here for the rest of my life . . ." Jen paused as she looked out to the girls in the store. ". . . with them."

"That's not true. You're so smart, and you're still young. You have plenty of time to figure out what you want to do," Reagan encouraged her.

"Thanks, girl. I don't know how to explain it. I think I'm afraid I'm gonna wake up one morning at forty-five years old and have no career, no life, and no family."

Reagan shut her locker and closed the lock. "I really think it'll be all right. You're worrying too much."

Jen shrugged and closed her locker, too. She and Reagan made eye contact for a moment then Jen spoke. "Let's do this."

They stood back-to-back at their respective registers, cherishing the last five minutes of freedom before opening time. Reagan glanced at her watch a couple of times, as if doing so would make the time go faster.

"How was your weekend, anyway?" Jen asked her.

"You know, library, reading, loneliness . . ." Reagan started her usual response, then she paused, remembering the one difference. "Actually, there was one thing."

"Oh, yeah?"

"Yeah, you remember that guy on Friday? The one that you said liked me?"

"Sure, that hot guy that was dying to talk to you?" Jen asked.

"Yeah him. Well, he kinda bumped into me outside the library on Saturday."

"Really?"

"I walked out and started down the sidewalk and he just came up and started talking to me," Reagan said.

"Uh-huh. I knew he liked you." Jen thought for a second. "You think he was following you?"

"No, I'm pretty sure he was just across the street and saw me."

"Oh, well that's a relief," Jen said with a grin.

"Trust me, I will never have a stalker," Reagan said. "Who

would want to stalk this?" She pointed to her face, then dragged her hand down to her legs, as if she was a display on a game show.

Jen started laughing. "Why are you so hard on yourself? You're really pretty; don't you see that?"

"I mean, no one's ever noticed me, so . . ."

"Reagan, I'm sure guys have noticed you. Maybe they didn't say anything, but that doesn't mean they didn't notice you. And anyway, guys change a lot when they grow up. When they're kids, they don't always have the best judgment."

"I guess."

"Trust me," Jen said. "Your biggest weakness isn't the way you look, it's your lack of confidence."

Reagan smiled back at Jen. "Thanks, I suppose you're right. It's something I need to work on I guess."

The girls dragged themselves through the workday, both motivated by the need for a payday. The camaraderie they had with each other helped make the time a little easier. Every day felt like deja vu. They worked with the same self-centered group of girls, helping countless strangers pick out their clothes and accessories. The citizens of Newbrook had found the means necessary to shop for Christmas. That, or they spent money they didn't have. Either way, the business kept Reagan occupied.

It was nearly one and Reagan was getting ready to take her break. Jen insisted that she go ahead and go, even though there were a few customers in line. Reagan turned to walk away.

"Reagan," Jen whispered. "Reagan," she said, louder the second time.

Reagan turned around.

"What?" she asked Jen, but it didn't take her long to see why her friend had called her name.

Jackson had walked in the door, and this time he was alone.

She looked away from him and walked back over to Jen. "Oh God, what do I do?"

"Just be normal. It's okay. He's probably here to see you."

"Yeah, that's what I'm worried about," Reagan said nervously.

"That's a good thing," Jen said, smiling. "Be cool. Keep working and act like you didn't see him."

"You want me to ignore him?"

"No, not really. I just mean, don't make a big deal of it."

"Okay. All right," Reagan muttered before taking a deep breath. She stood back at the counter and started helping a customer, while keeping a mental note of where he was.

He surveyed the small selection of men's cologne near the counter and Reagan struggled to ignore the fact that he was only a few feet away. She wasn't the only one that was keeping an eye on him, though. Valerie already had him on her radar and was boasting to Tina and Beth that he had come back to talk to her again.

Jackson looked over at Reagan at the counter, as she was finishing up with her customer. He appeared unsure of what to say. But soon enough, he was given a gentle nudge to speed up the process, as Valerie was on her way over. He snatched up the bottle closest to his right hand and stepped toward the counter. Reagan looked up at him and smiled.

"Hello again," he said to her.

"Oh, hi." She spoke as if she was clueless about his existence there. "Some cologne this time?" she asked. *Duh, of course he's getting cologne, Reagan.*

"Hey, Jackson!" Valerie shrieked from right next to him.

Jen rolled her eyes from her counter.

"Hey," he mumbled, without giving her the slightest glance. He kept eye contact with Reagan and ignored Valerie's presence. "Yeah, I saw this bottle the other day, but I didn't know if I wanted to get it or not."

"Well, it's a good choice. It's one of our best sellers," Reagan told him.

Valerie turned up the flirtatiousness, leaning on the counter and tucking her hair behind her ear. "I bet that will smell great on you," she told him.

Jen stuck her finger in her mouth, practically gagging herself at Valerie's desperation. He paused for a second, appearing uncomfortable with the actions of the annoying girl at his side. Reagan glanced at Valerie for a moment, then looked back at Jackson, who was growing visibly frustrated.

"Um, that's sixteen ninety-eight," Reagan told him.

"All right." He pulled out his wallet, grabbed a twenty-dollar-bill, and handed it to her.

Reagan opened the register and exchanged the necessary bills. "Three-o-two is your change. Here you go," she said, handing him the bag.

"Thanks." He stood there for a second and smiled at Reagan, until his patience finally ran out and he turned to Valerie. "Can I help you?" he asked her, rather politely.

The look on her face displayed her shock, as she had never received this kind of response before.

"Um, no, I just wanted to see if you needed anything," Valerie replied in a lower octave.

"I'm good. Thank you, though," he said.

"No problem," Valerie muttered before walking back to Beth and Tina. They were waiting for her in the women's section.

Jen smiled from ear to ear and continued to check out customers on the other side. Reagan watched Valerie walk away and refrained from laughing. Jackson focused his attention back on Reagan.

"Listen, uh, would you like to hang out sometime?"

Reagan blushed and began to stutter. "Um . . . uh . . ."

"I'm sorry, I shouldn't have . . ." he started.

"It's okay," she said.

"No. I shouldn't have done that. You don't even know me.

I'm sure what you want is some strange guy bombarding you at work," he said, looking nervous.

"I'd love to," Reagan said boldly.

His head snapped up and he looked at her in shock. "Okay. Uh, what do you like to do? Where do you wanna go?"

"Oh, I'm not picky. I like about anything."

"All right. So, I'm betting hanging out at the mall is out of the question, huh? I doubt you want to be here when you aren't working," he said.

"Actually, I don't mind. As long as I'm not in here," she answered.

He laughed at her response. "Okay. Well, maybe we can just walk around or something. Do you work Saturday?"

"No, I usually only work on weekdays."

"So, how's Saturday then? Will that work?" he asked.

"Yeah, that'll be good," she said.

"Okay, you wanna meet in the food court around noon? We can grab a bite to eat, walk around, whatever you want to do."

"Sure, that sounds great."

"Awesome. All right. Uh, I guess I'll see you Saturday then?" he asked again.

"I'll be here," she said.

He walked away with a smile and headed out into the mall. Reagan decided to take a breath, for almost the first time since he entered the store.

Jen whipped around immediately. "Holy shit, Reagan. That was the greatest thing I've ever seen. It's adorable how hard he was trying to talk to you. And the way he blew off Valerie . . . hilarious!"

"Shhh, I don't wanna make a big deal out of it," Reagan said, looking around.

"I know, I'm sorry. I'm just so happy for you. And you have to admit, what he did was . . ."

"Um, what was that, Reagan?" Valerie asked, as the trio walked up to the counter.

"What was what? What did I do?" Reagan asked.

"You totally tried to keep me from talking to Jackson. Who do you think you are, anyway?"

"I don't know what you're talking about. I didn't do anything."

"Do you honestly think he's gonna pick you over me?" Valerie snipped. "You're, you're, well you're you. He'll never go out with someone like you."

"I didn't . . . he just . . ." Reagan stammered.

"Leave her the hell alone, Valerie. You're just pissed 'cause he blew you off. Get over yourself," Jen said, stepping toward Valerie.

Valerie looked at Jen and laughed. "You're as bad as she is. A couple weirdos." She walked away, Beth and Tina following right behind her.

"Bye," Jen spouted at her back. She turned toward Reagan and chuckled. "Don't worry about her. She has nothing on you."

"I know, but I don't get it. I've never done anything to her," Reagan said, shrugging.

"Nope, she's just a bitch. All there is to it," Jen said.

Reagan eventually took her break, and the other girls didn't bother her anymore. She watched the clock drag on until it was finally time to leave. Jen gave her some final words of encouragement, then she headed out for the night, dreading the fact that she had to come back the next day.

When she got home, Reagan immediately took off her winter gear and flopped down on the couch. She was still in disbelief at her conversation with Jackson. Her heart fluttered as she sat there and replayed the experience in her mind, over and over. A malicious grin spread across her face when she remembered how he had ignored Valerie. It was refreshing to see someone put her in her place.

She'd never been on a real date before, and she didn't even know if that's what this would be. All she knew was she was scared to death. *What will I talk about? Why is he even talking to me at all?* The thoughts raced through her head, until she finally made herself get up to find something to eat. Eventually, she curled up in the chair and opened her newest book. The pages of this one were all starting to blur together, as Reagan's mind kept floating off into a daydream. She finished an entire chapter and had no clue what she had just read. This week was sure to be the longest she had experienced in a long time.

CHAPTER 4

Saturday morning finally arrived, after what seemed like a month of waiting. Reagan started the weekend like any other; she ate her breakfast, got dressed, and headed to the library. But she had a little extra pep in her step when she walked through the door, and it didn't take Donna long to notice.

"Well, good morning, Reagan. You seem energetic this morning. The book must have been good, huh?"

Reagan smiled. "Yes, it was. I finished it last night." She stood at the counter, trying not to seem awkward but, the more she tried to hide it, the more it showed.

"Is there something else?" Donna asked.

"No . . . well, sort of. It's nothing really," Reagan started. She looked into Donna's curious eyes, not sure how to even begin such a conversation. She had grown used to their discussions of fictional love stories, but talking about a real-life experience was something she had not done with Donna before. "So, about a week ago, this guy came into the store with his friends. He didn't say much then, but he came back again on Monday."

"And?"

"He asked me if I wanted to hang out with him."

"Ah, okay. So . . ." Donna began.

"You think it's weird? I don't even know him," Reagan said.

"Not necessarily. What's he wanting to do? I mean, he isn't wanting to meet you somewhere alone, is he?"

"No, no. He thought maybe we could walk around the mall or something," Reagan said.

"All right, that sounds reasonable. At least you know there will be other people around, in case he does turn out to be a creep." Donna noted the fear that had suddenly struck Reagan's face. "I'm joking, dear," she said playfully. "Yeah, that sounds harmless. So, is he cute?"

"Yes, he's gorgeous. That's what scares me the most." Reagan spoke the words that she had held in for days.

"Why?"

"Because . . . I don't know. 'Cause, he is good-looking and confident, and cool; basically, everything that I'm not." She rubbed her forehead, anxious about the situation.

"Wait a minute now. First of all, you are a beautiful girl. And do you think that because you're quiet and you like to read, that means you aren't desirable?" Donna asked.

"I don't know, I guess."

"Oh, honey. Things aren't like they were in high school."

"You're starting to sound like Jen," Reagan said.

"Well, it's true. Things change as you get older. At least for the most part."

"I'll take your word for it. I've never really been in this situation before."

"You're gonna be just fine. You won't be alone, so that's good. And you're just talking. If you don't like each other, then you just don't see him again," Donna said.

"And what if I like him, but he doesn't like me? Then what?" Reagan asked.

"I wouldn't worry about that right now. Just relax and have a good day and whatever happens, happens."

A smile reappeared on Reagan's face. "Thanks, Donna."

Reagan found herself a new book and Donna wished her luck as she headed out the door. Donna's words of encouragement were helpful, but Reagan was still struggling to build confidence in herself. As much as she appreciated her friends telling her that she was beautiful, she had convinced herself that they were merely the biased words of the only two buddies she had.

A couple of hours later, she parked her car in the mall parking lot and turned off the engine. She looked at the time on her watch, then tapped her fingertips on her thigh. Her nervous breaths started to fog up the driver's side window. She glanced at her watch again, only forty seconds later. With one more deep inhale, she opened the door and headed inside. The butterflies that had overcome her gut had her wondering if she was even going to be able to eat.

The mall was a lot busier than she was used to, although still skimpy for December. There were only two weeks left until Christmas and the last-minute shoppers were just getting started. She entered through a different entrance than normal, trying to avoid the store that caused her agony five days a week. Rarely did she see the rest of the building, as she usually left as fast as possible.

Reagan slowly weaved through the groups of people, taking in the sounds and smells around her. The scent of candles drifted from a nearby store, then the cinnamon rolls across the hall mixed in. She could see the food court ahead in the center of the building. All the peripheral hallways led to that focal point in the middle. There were ten or so restaurants to choose from and close to one hundred tables between them. They glowed in the spotlight of the sun beaming through the glass ceiling above.

And there he was. Jackson was sitting at one of the tables, alone. He was using one hand to pick at the fingernails on the other. His right knee bounced up and down as his heel left the floor over and over. Reagan slowed her pace and watched him from afar. His nervous appearance made her feel a little better. Perhaps it was the reassurance that she wasn't alone in her apprehension. She inched her way toward him, second-guessing her decision to be there.

Jackson lay both of his hands on his thighs, gazing around the room. His head lined up in her direction and it stopped. He squinted for a moment, struggling to see through the crowd, then he rose. Reagan grinned and continued toward him. She paused for a second to let a group of children pass between them, then took the last few steps.

"Good morning," Jackson said. He looked down at his watch. "Afternoon, actually."

"Have you been waiting long?" she asked.

"Nah, I've only been here ten minutes or so."

"That's good. So . . ." She looked around.

"Are you hungry?" he asked.

"Yeah, you?"

"Always," he replied. "So, what sounds good to you?"

"I like about anything. Sorry, I know that doesn't help."

"That's okay, me too. How about pizza?"

"Sounds great," she said.

They strolled over to Mama's Pizza Place and stood at the end of the line. Reagan remained quiet and Jackson seemed to sense her uneasiness.

"So, what's your favorite kind of pizza?" he asked her, breaking the ice.

"I love pepperoni and olives," she said. "I hate green peppers, but I'll eat about anything else."

"Same here. My favorite is pepperoni and sausage, but I'll eat whatever. As long as it doesn't have peppers and onions on it. Cooked onions kinda gross me out," he said.

"Oh yeah?"

"Yeah, I think it's 'cause they get kinda slimy. I don't know."

"I can understand that," Reagan said.

They continued their chit-chat until it was time for them to order.

"What can I get for you, dear?" the woman behind the counter asked Reagan.

"I'll take a slice of pepperoni, please," Reagan said. The choices were limited, with only a couple of different types available.

"Me too," Jackson added. He turned to Reagan as the woman plated their slices of pizza. "I'd like to pay if that's okay," he said.

"Thank you. You don't have to do that," she said, blushing.

"I know, but it's okay."

"Would you like something to drink?" the woman asked them.

"I'll take root beer, if you have it," said Reagan.

"Coke for me, please," Jackson said.

Jackson paid for their food and drinks, and the two walked to the cleanest table they could find. The decibel level in the room had picked up a little as more people had made their way to the mall.

"I'm really sorry that I suggested we meet here. I'm sure you'd rather go somewhere far away from work," Jackson said.

Reagan chewed her mouthful of cheese and pepperoni, shaking her head. "It's okay. I don't ever venture out into the mall, actually, so it's kinda nice."

"That's good. I was a little worried that you might be miserable."

Reagan chuckled and shook her head again.

Jackson ate for a minute before continuing the conversation. "So, you've worked here for a year, huh? Do you like it?"

She paused for a moment and took a drink. "Honestly . . . no."

"Oh, I'm sorry."

"It's alright, it's my fault," she said.

"What do you mean?" he asked.

"Well, I went to college, but I'm not using it."

"Oh, I see what you're sayin'. So, what did you major in?" he asked.

"Art and business."

"Really? Two degrees?

"Yeah, silly huh?" she said.

"No, not at all. That's awesome," he replied.

"Well, you know the story. I love to paint. So, I thought I could open my own store and sell my paintings," Reagan said.

"You should," Jackson told her. "That would be really cool."

"It will be, if I ever get to that point," she replied. "It would be more fulfilling to me than running the cash register at Katie's for the rest of my life."

"I doubt you'll be there your whole life," he encouraged her.

"I hope you're right."

"You won't," he reiterated.

"Thanks," she replied. She took the last couple bites of her pizza and another swig of her root beer, then looked across to Jackson. He had already finished his. "You want to walk for a little bit?" she asked.

"Yeah, sounds good to me."

The pair strolled up and down the halls, discussing whatever topics came to mind. Jackson seemed curious yet reserved about talking to Reagan. She felt like he was trying to make chit-chat, but there was an awkwardness about him, like he was unsure of what to talk about. They made their way through most of the mall, but there remained a barrier between them that neither knew how to take down.

"So, do you want something?" Jackson asked.

"Like what?" she asked, not sure what he meant.

"I don't know. Is there a shirt or something you want?" Jackson rephrased.

"No, not really. I don't need anything," she said. Reagan stopped walking and turned to face him. "Jackson, you don't have to buy me things or impress me. I don't care about that stuff."

"Okay, I'm sorry. I was just trying to be nice."

"I know, and I'm sorry if that sounded rude. I do appreciate it, but I don't want you to get the wrong impression about me." She held his gaze longer than she had up to this point, trying to convey her sincerity. He started to speak then stopped, peering at every last detail on her face. She grew uncomfortable and began fidgeting with her sweater. "What?" she asked him.

"Nothing, I've just never met a woman like you before."

"But you hardly know me yet," she said.

"I know. It's just a feeling I get."

"Maybe you haven't been around the right kind of women."

"You're right, I haven't," he said.

He glanced around at the crowds and Reagan continued to display uncomfortable body language. She had no clue how to read Jackson and, frankly, she was starting to feel like this was all a joke.

"Well, I think I better . . ." She trailed off.

Jackson waited a moment for her to continue, then decided to break the silence. "Have I done something?"

"No. I'm sorry, I'm just not very good at this," Reagan said, trying to hide the look of fear on her face.

"You're doing fine," he reassured her. "If I said something . . ."

"You haven't done anything. I'm just . . . I'm just awkward."

"No, that's the thing. You're real, and I'm not used to that," he told her.

"I'm nobody. That's . . ." She started speaking, then looked down at her sweater again. He opened his mouth to begin speaking and she decided to finish. "That's what worries me."

"What's worrying you? I don't understand," he said.

"I'm a nobody and you are a popular, good-looking guy.

What are you doing, talking to me? Is this a joke or a game? Did your friends think it would be funny?" She felt heat rising in her cheeks and she turned to walk away.

"No." He followed her and cut her off. "No, Reagan. No one put me up to anything and it isn't a joke. Why are you being so guarded?"

She looked away from him. "I don't know. I told you . . . I'm awkward. What can I say?"

"You don't trust me, right? Is that it?" he asked. She remained silent, watching the people pass by them in both directions. "Look, I don't blame you. Some strange guy approached you at work, out of nowhere, and asked you out to lunch. I'm sure it's a little weird. But I promise you, I'm not a creep and I'm not here to use you. I just thought you seemed, I don't know, different."

She raised a brow. "Different?"

"Yes, and I don't mean that in a bad way. What I mean is, you seemed mysterious. I can't explain it. It was a feeling I got the first time I saw you. You weren't fixated on yourself." He stopped talking and Reagan finally began to believe that maybe, just maybe, this guy was trustworthy. "I promise you. I don't want to hurt you or make you feel uncomfortable. I want to get to know you, that's it. Give me a chance. Then, if you decide that I'm revolting or creepy or just plain weird, then I'll leave you alone."

Reagan managed to smile up at him and he gave her one in return.

"Okay," she whispered.

"Listen, I had a good time today," he said. "I'd really like to see you again, but only if you want to and whenever you're comfortable."

She thought for a moment, letting all her senses help her form her next words. "How about tomorrow?" she asked.

Jackson's eyes widened in disbelief. "Yeah, that's great. What time? What do you want to do? Probably not the mall, right?"

"Um . . ." she started.

"I'm joking," he added with a smile. "Seriously, you name it. Anything."

"Do you like Christmas lights?" she asked.

CHAPTER 5

Reagan and Jackson had made plans to spend Sunday evening together. One of the Christmas traditions in Newbrook was the display of lights that stretched on for blocks in the heart of downtown. Most of the citizens would make their way to the exhibition every year, even though it rarely changed. It was one of the few things that people could do and not spend a dime more than the gas it took them to get there. Lucky for Reagan, the display was only six blocks from her apartment. Jackson drove across town to meet her by the library.

Reagan layered up in her winter gear, then walked out the door and down the steps. She wasn't quite as nervous as she had been at the mall, but convincing herself to trust this guy she barely knew was a challenge for her. She started down the sidewalk, each breath forming a cloud that seemed to linger in the air for an eternity. Jackson was there ahead of her, standing on the sidewalk alone.

"Waiting on me again, I see," Reagan joked.

Jackson pulled his hands out of his pockets and shrugged his shoulders. "Hey, what can I say?"

"I'm sorry," she said.

"No worries. You ready for this?"

"Definitely."

Hundreds of thousands of bulbs glowed brightly enough that drivers could easily travel without their headlights as they passed by. Nearly twenty square blocks had been decorated with a variety of trees, strands of lights, and nativity scenes. No one was sure how many plastic Santas and reindeer were mixed throughout the arrangement. In the end, it all came together to make the perfect homogeneous assortment.

"Wow! Look at this," Jackson said.

"I know, isn't it great? I came over here last year, too. Almost makes you feel like it's part of a fairy tale, doesn't it?"

"Yeah, it does. I forgot how neat it was. I used to come with my family when I was young, but . . . well, it's been a while since I've seen it," he told her.

"Oh, that sucks. Why not?" Reagan asked.

Jackson ran his left hand through his dark hair and looked down at Reagan. "Uh . . ." he started.

"Sorry, I shouldn't be so nosy."

"No, it's okay. Well, when I was nine, my mom left. After that, it was just me, my brother, and my dad. Everything sort of changed, I guess."

"I'm so sorry. I shouldn't have . . ." Reagan started.

"It's all right. No worries. I figured we'd talk about it eventually. Just came up a little sooner than I expected, that's all."

Reagan grew quiet, unsure of what she should say next. They kept walking and Jackson continued.

"When I was young, I didn't understand what was happening, and I still don't even know why she left. I just remember she always seemed, I don't know, unhappy, I guess. She was there and we would talk to her, but she wasn't really there, if you know what I mean."

Jackson paused for a minute. He avoided eye contact with her, looking out into the lights. Reagan waited on him to resume.

"I felt so many things for so long – anger, confusion, sadness . . . But most of all, I felt sorry for my dad and my brother, Dallas.

He was only five, damn it. He needed his mother. And my dad, my poor dad. She left him alone with two lost little boys. He stayed strong for us, but I knew when he went to bed at night, he would cry."

By this point, Reagan had teared up, as any human would when hearing this. She dabbed at the bottom of her eyes with her royal blue glove. The combination of the cold air and the water-works caused her nose to run. She compulsively sniffed to keep it from draining. Jackson heard the tiny sniffle and looked down at Reagan.

"Hey, it's all right. I'm sorry, I didn't mean to upset you," he said.

"I'm okay, I just feel terrible for you. And listen to you apologizing to me," she replied, shaking her head.

"I feel like an idiot. We're here to look at Christmas lights, and you're stuck listening to me, like I'm in counseling."

"You can talk about it if you want. I don't mind. I'm just sorry I made you think about it."

"It's all right. I mean it," he insisted.

Reagan nodded and they kept going. She eventually spoke up. "So, tell me something else about yourself."

"What do you want to know?"

"Anything, I guess."

"Okay, let's see here." He clapped his hands together and rubbed them back and forth. "Well, my favorite color is green, unless it's a green bean, 'cause I hate green beans. I went to college for one year, but I just didn't feel like I was ready for it yet. I didn't know what I wanted to be, so I came home to work at dad's construction company, at least until I could figure some things out. I couldn't see getting a degree for the sake of having one, then wondering if I even liked what I went for in the first place."

"That's completely understandable, and it was a good decision," Reagan encouraged him.

"I hope so."

"So, you work for your dad?"

"Yeah. Well, it probably doesn't seem like it, since I've been hangin' around the mall, but usually, he keeps me busy. We were kind of slow, so I took a few days off," he explained.

"That makes sense," she said.

He continued. "What else? Other than basketball and swinging a hammer, I have zero talents."

Reagan smiled. "All right, so what's your favorite food? You said you hate green beans. What food do you like?"

"Oh, wow, that's tough. I love to eat, so this is hard, but I'll have to go with my dad's chili," he said.

"Really?" Reagan replied, not expecting his response.

"Yeah, it's so good, trust me. What's yours?"

"That's tough for me, too. I love seafood. But I'd have to say lasagna, I guess."

"Good one. Love it," Jackson said.

"It's hard to pick one, 'cause I like about any Italian pasta, but lasagna has to be my favorite. Of course, that depends on who makes it. My mom's is so good, 'cause she adds a layer of pepperoni in it." she added.

"That does sound good." Jackson paused for a second as they continued walking. "So, do your parents live in town?

"No. They live about two hours from here. It's definitely drivable, but I can't just stop by whenever I feel like it," she replied. "I came here to go to school, and I just stayed when I was done, trying to start a life of my own." She shrugged her shoulders and forced a smile.

"You don't seem like you're too thrilled about it," he commented.

"Ugh, I don't know. I like it here and all, but I do miss them. I think it would be better if I felt like I was doing something with my life, but I don't. I don't have any friends, other than the librarian and one girl I work with. I don't like my job very much, but I have to save money if I want to open a store one day. And I can't really do it in my hometown, 'cause it just isn't big enough to be successful. So, I'm kinda stuck. But at least there are more people here. And with a bigger city nearby, there's at least a chance, right?"

"Yeah, I think it'll do great," he encouraged her. "But it kinda sucks that you aren't happy in the meantime. Just 'cause you're trying to save money, doesn't mean that you can't live while you wait."

Reagan laughed and looked up at Jackson. "I spend every Saturday morning of my life at the library, finding another book to read on the weeknights after I get home from work. And on the weekends, I paint. That's really about all I do."

"Well, that's okay. There are a lot worse things you could do."

"Yeah, that's true, I guess," she said, smiling.

The two had meandered around the end of the light display and started back up the other side. Both of them were much more comfortable than they had been the previous day. Reagan was learning to open up to this mysterious man, who seemed to be interested in her. She still didn't quite understand why a guy with so many friends was willingly hanging out with a girl like her. But for now, she was trying to follow her gut.

They were approaching their turn back to the library when a man and woman began walking toward them from the restaurant across the street. Reagan noticed the pair and gave them a quick glance, not thinking anything of it. Jackson, on the other hand, appeared noticeably uncomfortable at seeing the advancing duo. He looked away from them and continued forward.

"What's wrong?" Reagan asked.

Before Jackson could answer, the guy in the street spoke up. "Jackson?"

"Hey, man. What's goin' on?" Jackson replied.

The man looked at Jackson, then down at Reagan, and it was at that moment that she realized who he was. She made brief eye contact with Jackson's friend from the store, then quickly looked down at her toes.

He looked back to Jackson and smirked. "What are you doin'?"

"Just hangin' out," Jackson said, nodding.

"O . . . kay," his friend replied. He looked at the woman standing next to him and the pair smiled at each other, as if fighting the urge to laugh.

After an agonizing moment of awkward silence, Jackson spoke up. "Well, we better get going."

His friend smiled again and shrugged his shoulders. "Yeah. I'll see ya around then."

"See ya," Jackson replied quickly.

The two couples went their separate ways. Reagan tried to ignore the snide comments coming from the direction of the two walking away. She and Jackson strolled quietly on towards the library. The tone of their evening had suddenly changed, and Reagan's gut was no longer unquestioning.

Jackson put his hands in his pockets and stopped at the bottom of the library steps. "Look . . . I, uh . . ."

Reagan, who tended to follow another's lead in a conversation, knew exactly what she wanted to say. The words were leaving her mouth before she had a chance to second-guess herself. "I had a really good time, Jackson, but maybe we shouldn't see each other again."

"What? Why?"

"Come on. You know why," she said.

"Is it because of Drew? I'm sorry, he's not very nice sometimes. Don't worry about him . . ."

"No, it's because of you," Reagan replied sternly.

Jackson's face expressed confusion. "But I . . ."

"Your friend being a jerk isn't the problem. The problem is, the way you freaked out when you saw him. It's the way you avoided eye contact with him when he saw me. You were embarrassed to be seen with me, weren't you?" she asked.

"No, Reagan . . ."

"Don't lie to me, Jackson!" she said. "He showed up and you panicked. Just admit it."

He rubbed his forehead and continued to stutter, "I don't . . . he's not . . ."

"What?" she demanded. "Just say it."

"You're right, I'm sorry. He's been my friend since we were in the fourth grade, but he didn't start acting this way until he got his new job. Now, it's like he thinks he's better than everybody."

"I told you, he isn't the problem. He is who he is. But if you are embarrassed to be with me, then we don't need to spend time together."

"But I'm not . . ." he started.

"You're not what?"

"I'm not embarrassed of you," he stated a little louder. "I just didn't feel like hearing his crap."

"Then why do you keep hanging out with him? If you don't like how he treats people, then why not stop being his friend?"

"I don't know. It's complicated. We've been friends for so long."

"Well, I don't know him, and I really don't even know you yet, but it doesn't look like he's much of a friend," she said.

He looked down and nodded.

"Look," she continued. "It's none of my concern what kind of friendship you guys have. I'm nobody and I definitely don't expect you to change your life or be uncomfortable because of me."

"But you don't make me uncomfortable," he said, stepping toward her. "You're amazing and beautiful. You are real, and I'm just a coward. You're right, I shouldn't have let him act that way. I should have stood up for myself, and you. I don't know why I didn't. I'm just scared, I guess."

"Scared of what?"

"I don't know. Scared of not fitting in, maybe."

"What's so bad about being different?" Reagan asked. "You said it yourself, it takes courage. And it's a challenge, no doubt.

But I would much rather be different and be me, than be like everyone else and not know who I am."

Jackson stepped up to her, reached his right hand up to her dishwater blonde hair, and pulled her lips into his. They held their kiss for a moment before he stepped back and stared down at her. She looked back up at him, trying to read his eyes, his expression. She quivered from the cold and the pounding in her chest, her nose red from enduring the temperature for so long.

"I'm sorry," he said, waiting on her to respond. Her silence seemed to make him uneasy. "Say something, please."

"Why did you do that?" she asked him.

"Because you amaze me. I had to, I'm sorry."

"I'm not," she replied.

He smiled at her and she gave him one in return.

"Reagan, I would really like to see you again. I don't blame you if you say no 'cause, after tonight, I don't deserve your company, but . . ."

"I'd love to," she interrupted him.

"Great. Okay, you name it. Anything you want to do."

She stood for a moment, thinking. "Well, there's a movie coming out next weekend that I'd like to see if you're up for it," she suggested.

"Just tell me when and where to pick you up."

Jackson walked her the last couple blocks to her apartment building. She exchanged phone numbers with this man, who had still managed to melt her heart, despite the doubt she had felt.

"I had a good time," he told her. "I'm sorry for what happened. I promise it won't happen again."

She smiled and nodded. "Thank you. And I'm sorry for being nosy earlier."

"Nah, no worries. How could you have known?"

She twiddled her thumbs for a moment and looked at the door. "Well, I'm gonna hit the hay. Gotta go to work tomorrow."

"Eww, I forgot tomorrow is Monday," he said in disgust.

"Yeah," she replied.

He hesitated before spitting out his next words. "Good night, Reagan."

He leaned in and kissed her on the cheek, then pulled back enough to make eye contact. She held her position, letting him know it was okay. This time, he went for her lips. They held each other for the longest moment of her life, until he pulled back again.

"Good night, Jackson," she said.

He backed away slowly, smiling from ear to ear, watching Reagan climb to the door. She gave him one last glance, then closed the door behind her.

CHAPTER 6

At the mall on Monday morning, Reagan updated Jen on everything that happened throughout the weekend.

"So, you're seeing him again?" Jen asked in excitement.

"Yeah, Saturday. We're goin' to the movies."

"That'll be fun, huh."

"God, I don't know what to think. Is this really happening? Am I crazy, Jen? I don't wanna let myself get hurt by a guy who's ashamed to be seen with me. What am I thinking?" she asked.

"I don't think he's ashamed of you, Reagan. Maybe he's never been in this situation or felt this way before," Jen suggested. "He might just be a little confused."

"Yeah, I suppose. Only time will tell, I guess. In the meantime, I'll just go with it."

"I would. Sounds pretty nice to me," Jen said, winking.

Reagan grinned at Jen. "I'll say it again. That's what worries me."

The two worked their way through the morning, and the time crawled at snail speed for Reagan.

Only Tina and Valerie were on the floor, most likely because Beth didn't feel like getting out of bed. The girls weren't quite as energetic when their trio wasn't complete. But on this day, Valerie appeared to have other concerns besides her missing friend, and she had her eye on Reagan. For the first time since her initial day on the job, Reagan was giddy and cheerful, and Valerie was reserved.

At lunchtime, Jen made her way to the breakroom, while Reagan covered the cash register. Valerie jumped on the opportunity to question Reagan, now that she was flying solo. She waited until the line dwindled, then snaked her way over to the counter to face the woman that she had stewed about all day. Reagan couldn't help but notice her approaching.

Valerie leaned against the counter and lay her arms across the top, smirking at Reagan. "I saw you at the mall on Saturday," she said.

"Yeah?" Reagan replied.

"What do you think you're doing?"

"I don't know what you're talking about."

"Oh, give me a break. I saw you walking with Jackson," Valerie said.

"So what? What's your problem, anyway?"

"Please, do you seriously think he's interested in someone like you?"

"He doesn't seem too interested in you," Reagan boldly replied. Her heart started pounding. A comment like this was far outside her comfort zone.

"Oh, really? Listen here, bitch. Jackson will never be with you. He's up here . . ." Valerie lifted her right hand as high as it would go. ". . . and you are down here," she said, as her left hand smacked the counter.

Tina glanced up from the back of the room, squinting in the direction of the sound. She decided to find work a little closer to the commotion.

The satisfaction that Reagan felt showed with the grin on her face. "You're jealous, aren't you?" she asked.

Valerie chuckled nervously. "Jealous of you? Keep dreaming, dork."

"What's going on?" Jen asked Valerie, as she approached.

"Nothing, we're just talking," Valerie answered her. It was apparent that Jen's dominant nature intimidated Valerie. "That was a fast break," Valerie sassed.

"Yeah, it's hard to relax back there with you out here, flappin' your jaw," Jen remarked.

Reagan started to laugh then stopped, clearing her throat.

"Whatever," Valerie said. She glared at Reagan one last time, then turned away toward Tina.

"Thanks," Reagan told her friend.

"No problem," Jen said. "What started that?"

"I guess she saw us at the mall the other day."

"Oh, she's just jealous."

"Yeah, it's all right. I think it's kinda funny, actually," Reagan said.

Jen laughed. "I know, right?"

Reagan finished out the day without another word from Valerie. Her irate coworker wouldn't even make eye contact with her. That entire week, Reagan drifted through each day in a daze, happy to feel like she had the upper hand for once. For her, it was torture waiting for Saturday to come. She hadn't been out to see a movie in years. Normally, she waited for them to come out on DVD so she could just watch them at home.

On Saturday morning, she made her usual trip to the library to exchange books and talk to Donna. Once again, Reagan had so much that she wanted to say, and none of it was about the book she had read. Donna, of course, enjoyed the chance to have a little girl talk, as Mary wasn't much of a chatter.

Around ten-thirty or so, Reagan headed back home to wait until it was time for Jackson to pick her up. The movie didn't start until two, and the next few hours were agonizing. There wasn't much variety in her small wardrobe, so the process of picking out what to wear was rather simple. This left her entirely way too much time to do nothing. She settled on throwing on a movie, despite where she was getting ready to go. Whatever it took to make the time pass by.

About the time the credits started to roll, Reagan heard knocking. She flipped the TV off and headed over to the foyer. After taking one last deep breath and peeping out to ensure that it was him, she turned the knob and opened the door. Jackson stood there, sporting a nice button-up and an even nicer smile.

"Hey," Reagan said.

"Hi," he replied. "I'm a little early. I hope that's okay."

"Of course. You wanna come in?"

"Sure, thanks." He walked in, barely clearing the door, then stopped. Reagan shut it behind him. "Nice place," he told her.

"Thanks. It's small, but it's just me, so it works out fine. And I can afford it, even on my meager salary."

Jackson chuckled. "Hey, I admire you. You're out here, making it on your own. I had my own place for a while, but I'm back with dad for now."

"Well, that's okay," she replied, smiling.

"I was doin' all right on my own, don't get me wrong. After Dallas went to college, dad started gettin' lonely by himself. So, I figured I'd move back in for a while. You know what I mean?"

"That's understandable. And it was very nice of you to help your dad like that. I'm sure he's grateful to have you there with him."

"Yeah, I think he is, when we're not arguing. I'll go eventually, but I wanna make sure he's all right first," he added. "Anyway, enough about me."

Reagan waited in silence for a moment, trying to think of what to say next. "You want a pop or somethin'?"

"Yeah sure. Thanks."

"No problem," she said as she headed into the kitchen. "I only got root beer. Is that all right?"

"That's great." He glanced over to the corner of the living room, as Reagan opened the refrigerator. She had turned the whole section into her art space. He examined what he could until she reentered the room.

"Here ya go," she said.

"Thanks. Ya mind if I check out your stuff?" he asked.

"No, go for it."

They walked over to the area that she had designated for painting. An entire collection of finished pieces lined the wall. An equally large number of blank canvases sat in a stack, having yet to see the stroke of a brush. A small bookshelf held her stock of brushes and paints. And, in the center of it all, was an old easel sitting upon a tarp that was speckled with a variety of colors.

"These are amazing, Reagan," Jackson stated with sincerity.

"Thank you. I keep piling them up, hoping they sell one day."

"Oh, I guarantee they will. They're all great."

"I appreciate it."

He walked up to the nearest painting, examining the landscape she had created. "Is this . . . what kind of paint is this?" he asked awkwardly. "Sorry, I don't know much about art."

"No, it's okay. It's acrylic. Kind of like house paint, but more expensive."

Jackson laughed and nodded. "Yes, and more beautiful."

"Yeah, that's true. I like painting with oils, too, but acrylic's a little easier to clean up. And watercolor and I don't get along, for some reason. I think it's beautiful, but I'm not that great at it. So, I stick with acrylic."

"Well, it's super cool, that's for sure."

Jackson continued to check out Reagan's collection of art, seeming to forget what he came there for in the first place. He finally stopped for a moment and looked at his watch. "Oh, it's one-thirty already. You wanna head over there?"

"Yeah, let me get my coat," Reagan replied.

Jackson chugged the rest of his root beer and put the can in her recycling bin before they headed out the door. He led the way to his car, a black Camaro, which he had parked across the street.

"Nice car," Reagan told him.

"Thanks. I got it a few months ago. I had to save forever to get it, but it was worth it."

"Definitely. It's a lot cooler than my little lemon."

"I bet yours gets a lot better gas mileage, though," he said.

Reagan laughed, as she was climbing in the passenger side. "Yeah, I suppose so."

He started the car, and the rumble of the engine echoed off the walls of the neighboring buildings. They started down the road. It was a short drive to the theater, yet it was much better than walking in the cold. With only six screens, the little cinema wasn't much, but they had great popcorn, cold drinks, and cheap movies. The convenience of this indoor, relatively low-cost activity meant that the seats were usually nearly full. Jackson had wisely prepared for this in advance, though. He had purchased their tickets days ahead of time.

They pulled into the small parking lot behind the building and climbed out into the chilly air. Jackson locked the car and they hurried toward the front door. The main lobby was warm and cozy, especially this time of year. Of course, the maroon carpet had seen better days, but the Christmas decorations compensated for that. They handed their tickets to the man who was collecting them, before wandering to the counter to get snacks.

"What can I get for you today?" the woman behind the counter asked.

Jackson looked over at Reagan. "You go ahead."

"I kinda want popcorn, but I can't really eat that much," she told Jackson.

"We can share one if you want," he suggested.

"Sure, that'll work. You wanna share some peanut M&Ms, too?"

"Mmm, yeah. They're my favorite," he answered.

He looked at the woman, who was patiently waiting on their decision. "Can we get a large popcorn, a box of peanut M&Ms, a medium Coke for me, and . . ."

"A small root beer for me, please," Reagan said.

Jackson paid for their snacks and they stood off to the side for a moment as they waited. Reagan admired the lights and ornaments that lined the room. Holiday music played softly in the background. She felt serenity in the festive surroundings. Jackson looked at Reagan as she smiled at the colorful setting. He looked at her hair. The natural highlights streaked backward into the clips that held the strands in place. His gaze moved to her face. He watched her soft lips and hazel eyes. Reagan finally sensed his stare and looked up at him.

"What?" she asked, growing uncomfortable.

"Nothing," he answered with a grin.

"What? Do I have something on my face?" She started wiping her forehead.

"No. Why . . .?" he started to ask her something.

"Here you go. Enjoy your movie," the woman said, handing them their food and drinks.

"Thanks," the pair replied in unison.

Jackson clutched the popcorn, Reagan picked up the chocolate, and they stepped away from the concessions.

"Uh," Reagan said, looking at her ticket stub. "We're in number four," she told him.

"All right," he replied.

They walked down the hallway until they reached the appropriately marked door. He pulled it open for her and she led the way into the dark room. Step by step, they descended into the theater.

"Where do you want to sit?" she asked him.

"Doesn't matter to me."

"Okay." She found a couple of seats in the middle, hoping to avoid dealing with people needing to squeeze through every five minutes. Jackson sat down and Reagan lay her coat on her seat. "I'm gonna run to the restroom real quick, while I have a chance."

"All right."

When she returned, Jackson was sitting there, watching the fun facts and movie trivia. Polite by nature, he had waited to start the popcorn until she came back.

"You didn't miss much," he told her.

"Okay, that's good." She sat down and looked up at the screen.

He waited a moment before he decided to speak. "Hey, why did you do that out there?"

"Do what?"

"Why did you assume there was something wrong when you saw me looking at you?" he asked. Reagan blushed and looked at her lap. "Like that. Why do you do that?"

"I don't know. I usually assume the worst, I guess."

"Why?" he asked again.

"Well, I'm not used to someone looking at me, unless it's to laugh at me. I've dealt with it my whole life. It's made me paranoid, I suppose," she answered with a shrug.

"Okay, first of all, I have no clue why anyone would ever laugh at you. You're beautiful and smart. And second, I was definitely not looking at you in a bad way. I was just looking at you."

"But why?"

"'Cause you . . . you astound me. There's just something about you that draws me in. I want to be around you. I want to talk to you and learn more about you. I want to hear your voice."

He stopped, gazing down at her fixated stare. "It's hard to explain," he finished and looked back up at the screen.

For the first time, Reagan didn't doubt whether he had good intentions. She didn't feel scared. She felt more joy than she had ever felt in her life.

Now she found herself fighting back tears to reply, "Thank you."

He smiled at her and grabbed her hand. "You're welcome."

She nodded, still enduring the burning sensation in her nose and eyes. "I feel the same way," she added.

"You do?" he asked.

"Yes, of course." Reagan noticed the look of relief on his face. "Did you think that I didn't like you?"

"Well, I was hoping that you did, but I thought I ruined it last weekend."

Reagan smiled up at him. "I wouldn't be here if I didn't like you, Jackson."

"I guess that's a good point," he said, grinning back at her.

Reagan and Jackson dug into the popcorn, talking like they'd known each other for years until the movie started. She found herself letting her guard down, quickly falling for a man that she didn't think she'd ever talk to, let alone have interested in her. Reagan still didn't understand why he had his eye on her, but she knew that he made her feel like she was perfect the way she was. This was something that she had doubted her entire life. Jackson held her close until the movie was over. They reluctantly stood up as the lights came back on.

"That was a good movie. Good choice," he told her.

"Thanks. I don't really remember much of it," she said. "But I'll take your word for it."

He chuckled at her comment. "Touché."

Reagan slung her jacket over her arm. They followed the mass of people out the door and started down the hallway toward the lobby. Jackson held her hand as they walked. They could barely get one foot in front of the other, making their way through the crowded hall. The couple inched their way forward until they could finally see the concession stand ahead. One last family stood in their way of reaching the opening. Jackson and Reagan excused themselves as they slid past the family, then a familiar face appeared before them. Once again, Jackson's friend Drew looked upon them, almost as if fated. But this time, Drew stood with a group of friends. They formed a cluster in the middle of the room, most certainly waiting for their turn to watch a movie.

Jackson continued forward with no hesitation and no sign of anxiety. Reagan, on the other hand, struggled to hide her apprehension. Her gaze dropped down toward the ugly carpet, then over toward the door. Inside, she hoped and prayed that they could just make it to the exit. But she wasn't going to get that lucky.

"Jackson, how's it goin'?" Drew asked obnoxiously.

"All right, man. You?"

Drew ignored Jackson's attempt to have a civil conversation and continued his mission to disturb the peace. "So, what is this, Jackson?"

Reagan's sweaty palms started to quiver, as her nerves kicked into high gear. Jackson squeezed her hand slightly, trying to reassure her that it would be okay.

"What are you talking about?" Jackson asked Drew in return, holding his ground.

"I just don't understand what you're doin', dude. You can have any chick you want. Why are you hangin' out with . . . with that?" Drew gestured toward Reagan.

She glanced down at her old clothes and examined what she could through the tears that had begun to well up in her eyes. Her shoes were speckled with paint. Her jeans had a couple of small spots to match and the hems at her feet were shredding as the cotton had aged. The flowered blouse she had picked out was what most might consider outdated, but it was practically brand new. Of course, it didn't show as much skin as the shirts on the girls in Drew's group. Reagan looked away and slipped her coat on.

Jackson's normally joyful expression had disappeared and was replaced with one of fury. He looked down at Reagan, who wouldn't even begin to lift her head, then back at Drew and his snickering posse.

"Oh, I get it, man. A piece of ass is a piece of ass, right?" Drew remarked.

Jackson immediately released Reagan's hand. He took one step with his left foot and swung at Drew's face with his right fist. Drew's limp body flew back into his cluster of friends, who suddenly had nothing to laugh at. A deafening silence filled the room and the only noise to be heard was the sound of Drew's moaning and the new popcorn exploding behind the counter. Drew climbed back to his feet, his hands over his face. A stream of blood was running down his neck, soiling his extravagant, flashy shirt.

Reagan now held her head high, and she couldn't believe what she was witnessing. She exchanged a glance with Drew, before looking up at Jackson. She didn't know what to think about what had just happened, but she knew without a doubt that her life was going to change.

"We're done," Drew mumbled through his hands.

Jackson grabbed Reagan's hand and strolled over to the manager behind the counter, who stared back at Jackson nervously.

"I apologize for all of this," Jackson said politely.

The middle-aged woman nodded in return. "It's all right, but you better go."

"Yes ma'am," he replied.

He glanced over at Drew one more time, then walked out the door with Reagan at his side.

The couple hurried along until they reached the car. Jackson's hand was now the one quivering, while Reagan felt rather calm. He unlocked the car and they both climbed in. Reagan didn't know what to say, or if she should even speak at all. She waited on him to take the lead.

"I'm so sorry, Reagan," he said. She shook her head, trying to tell him it was okay, but he continued. "No, I'm really sorry that you had to listen to that. Don't you listen to him. You're better than him. You're better than all of us."

He leaned across the stick shift and pulled her into a hug. Whether it was because of his heartfelt sorrow or the intensity of the situation, she wasn't sure. But her emotions began to flood her at once. Reagan cried and he held her with trembling arms.

CHAPTER 7

E mma's eyes widened, astonished by what her mother had told her. "Damn, dad was a badass!" Emma exclaimed.

"Emma," Reagan said, frowning at her daughter's choice of words.

"Sorry, but he was. I can't believe he did that."

"Believe it. I know he seems calm and quiet sometimes, but your father can be quite feisty when he needs to be."

Jackson walked in the door at that moment and both girls turned to look at him.

"Reagan, have you seen the watering can? These hanging pots are starting to get a little dry again."

"Look on the back porch, hon," Reagan told him.

"Thanks." He walked through the house and out the back door.

Emma raised her right brow, scrunching her face at her mom. "Are you sure you married the same guy?"

"Yes, I swear," Reagan said, laughing.

"Wow, that's seriously crazy. Why was dad friends with such a jerk in the first place?"

"Well, it's not always that easy. Sometimes things are okay between people in the beginning, but change over time. Your dad was just a kid when they became friends. Drew changed. It happens," Reagan said.

"Maybe dad changed, too," Emma suggested.

"Yes, I think you're right."

"Did dad ever talk to him after that?"

"No. We saw him from time to time, but your father had no interest in his friendship. And I'm sure Drew didn't either," Reagan added.

Emma stood up and walked over to the refrigerator to grab herself a pop. "You want one?" she asked her mother.

"Sure. Thank you."

Emma opened her can and took a big gulp, then she sat back down and handed her mom hers. "Well?"

"What?" Reagan asked.

"Go on. I'm sure there's more, right?"

"Oh, yes. Of course, your dad standing up for me like that meant the world to me. And it was a bit more action than I had ever seen before," Reagan said. Emma grinned and waited for her mother's next words. "Up to that point, there was always a little part of me that wondered if I was dreaming. And I had a huge trust issue. All of that went out the window that day, and I never doubted him again."

"And what about those bit . . . I mean, girls that you worked with? Did you keep having trouble with them, too?" Emma asked.

Reagan started laughing. "Funny you ask, actually. No, your dad put an end to that real quick, too." Emma looked a little scared. "Don't worry, he didn't hit any of them," Reagan joked. "He came into the mall one day while I was working, not too long after the theater thing. He strolled into the store, passing straight by Valerie. He gave her the evilest look, then kissed me right there in front of all of them."

"Seriously?" Emma said, nearly choking on her most recent swig.

"I'm dead serious."

"Oh, my God. That's hilarious! I bet Jen loved that."

"You have no idea. She said it was the best thing she had ever witnessed," Reagan replied, shaking her head.

"That's so crazy that you guys stayed friends after all these years," Emma said.

"Yeah, she's always had my back. She's a great friend. That was why I felt so terrible."

"Terrible about what?" Emma asked.

"Well, your dad wasn't the only big change in my life. It wasn't too long after this that I got a call from Donna."

"Oh, yeah. The lady from the library."

"Yes, but I guess I shouldn't get ahead of myself. I haven't told you about Christmas yet," Reagan added.

CHAPTER 8

R eagan got up early on Christmas morning, picked out a
festive sweater, and headed out the door, with her coffee
in one hand and a couple of presents in the other. Just like every
other day in December, she sat in the driver's seat, patiently
waiting for her car to warm up. She and Jackson had agreed to
spend Christmas morning with their respective families, then
spend time with each other later that evening. This meant that
Reagan had to leave by seven, so she would have plenty of time
with her mom and dad before returning home.

Even though Reagan was excited to visit her parents for the
first time in months, the thought of eating dinner later with
Jackson was the one thing she couldn't get off her mind. She was
both excited and nervous to tell her parents about him. After
two hours of driving, she still wasn't sure how she was going to
do it. She'd never really had such a conversation with them
before. To complicate it further, she didn't exactly know what to
tell them, considering she wasn't too sure of what their relationship was.

When she pulled into the driveway of her childhood home,
her mother, Barbara, was waiting at the open curtain in the
living room bay window. She smiled at the sight of her daugh-

ter's car. Reagan smiled and waved, then hopped out with the gifts and bolted into the house.

"Merry Christmas," her mother said, the moment the door opened.

"Merry Christmas, Mom," Reagan replied.

"Oh, it's so good to see you," her mother said, wrapping her up in a hug. "How was the drive?"

"Great. There weren't many people out. It was kinda nice," Reagan replied. She took her coat off and hung it on the hook next to the door. Then she slid her boots off and tucked them neatly beneath her hanging jacket. "Something smells good," she remarked, as she made her way to the tree to set the boxes down.

"Oh yes. That would be the pie . . . pecan, of course," her mom stated with pride.

"God, what time did you start cooking?" Reagan asked.

"Probably about the same time you left, I'd guess."

Reagan shook her head in disbelief. "You're amazing. You really didn't have to do all this."

"It's no trouble. I like having the chance to make a big meal," her mom insisted.

"Well, thank you. Is there anything I can help with?" Reagan asked.

"Maybe in a little bit. I'm gettin' ready to take this pie out. I'll probably stick the ham in shortly after, then we can open presents."

"Sounds good," Reagan said as she turned on the TV.

A few minutes later, Reagan's father, Tim, walked in. "Reagan! I didn't even hear you come in."

"Merry Christmas, Dad," Reagan said, standing up to hug him.

"Same to you, dear. I'm glad you made it." They sat down together on the couch. "So, how's work been goin'?" her dad asked.

"It's all right, I guess," she muttered with no enthusiasm.

"That good, huh?"

"I know, Dad. It's just temporary until I get enough money saved."

"I understand. What is it that makes it so . . . all right?" he asked.

"Actually, it's not that bad a job. But some of the girls I work with aren't very nice," Reagan said.

"I see."

"Except for one, Jen. She's cool. And the manager is okay. I don't see her a whole lot, but she's pretty nice. But the other three girls aren't my type at all."

"Well hang in there, honey. Hopefully, you won't be there much longer," he encouraged her.

"Yeah, I hope not."

Reagan and her father watched TV together for a few minutes, while her mother finished preparing the ham and getting it in the oven. Reagan found herself daydreaming while she tried to focus on the screen, wondering about Jackson and how his Christmas was going so far.

"You guys ready?" Barbara asked, walking into the living room.

"Ready when you are," Tim answered her.

"Alright, Santa. Put your hat on and get over to the tree," she told her husband.

Reagan laughed. "This will never get old."

Tim knelt next to the tree and examined the small pile of gifts. He read the name tag on the first one.

"Reagan, this is for you," he said. "Barbara," he continued. "Reagan . . . me . . . Reagan . . . Reagan . . . Barbara . . ." He carried on until he finished the last couple.

"You guys didn't need to get me this much stuff," Reagan told her parents.

"It's okay, dear. We're still gonna spoil you whenever we can," her mother insisted.

"Well, thank you," Reagan replied.

The family opened their gifts together in the sparkling glow from the big tree in the small living room. Christmas music, ripping paper, and chit-chat combined to raise the noise level in the tight quarters. Reagan gasped at her new paintbrushes, then held a couple of new blouses to her chest, demonstrating how they would look. Barbara's face lit up when she saw the mother's ring that her daughter had got for her. And Tim was equally excited to see his new cordless drill. When they were all finished, Reagan made her way into the kitchen to get a garbage bag for the paper. Barbara took advantage of the opportunity and reached for the hidden envelope in the tree. She sat next to Tim and waited for their daughter to walk back in.

When Reagan stepped back into the room, she immediately noticed her smiling parents on the couch. "What's goin' on?" she asked them.

"We have one more gift for you, hon," her mom said.

"O . . . kay," Reagan hesitated.

"We want you to have this," Barbara said.

Reagan took the envelope and gave her parents the "what did you do" look. The couple looked excited enough to jump off the couch. Reagan opened the envelope and pulled out the check that they had tucked inside.

"Five thousand dollars! Are you guys crazy? I can't take this," Reagan insisted. She felt emotional, looking at the valuable piece of paper.

"Now, before you get worried or upset, hear us out," her father said. "We've been puttin' money aside for you here and there for a while now. It's not as much as we wanted it to be, but we're hopin' it'll help you get your store started when you're ready."

Reagan wiped her tears away, followed shortly after by her mother wiping tears of her own. She held the check for a moment and took a deep breath, hoping to be able to speak a few words.

"Thank you so much," she finally said softly.

"You're very welcome, honey," her mother told her, standing

up to hug her daughter. They held each other for a few moments, then broke apart.

"This is so great. I can do so much with this!" Reagan exclaimed. "God, I can't wait to tell Jackson," she added.

"Tell who?" her mother asked.

Reagan felt like her heart stopped for a moment when she realized what she had said. She grinned back at her mom and glanced at her dad's curious face. "Um, actually I was gonna talk to you guys about this today. So . . . I met a guy. He came into the store a few weeks ago, when I was working. At first, he would try to talk to me and buy things for no reason. Then he asked me out one day. And we've had a couple of dates since."

"Really?" her mom asked with eagerness.

"I'm sorry I didn't tell you sooner. I kinda wanted to do it in person," Reagan said.

"Well, tell us a little about him," her dad pried for details.

"Okay. So, he's about a year younger than me. Really sweet, and smart. Tall, dark, and handsome. He works for his dad's construction company and hates green beans," Reagan said, chuckling to herself. "Honestly, I was amazed that he even noticed me."

"Why is that?" her mother asked.

"'Cause he's kind of always been the cool guy with lots of friends, and I'm, you know, not as cool."

"Oh, Reagan. You are a wonderful, special woman. As long as he sees that and likes you as you are, then it will be okay," Barbara said.

"I know. I feel a lot better about it now. It made me a little nervous at first, that's all," Reagan said.

"Nervous about what?" her dad asked.

"I don't know. I guess I was worried that it was all a cruel joke. Popular people have never really associated with me. And I know I'm a grown woman now and all that childish stuff shouldn't be a factor anymore, but sometimes it's hard to forget the way people treated me," Reagan said.

"Honey, I'd say you just keep following your instincts and everything will be okay," her mother advised.

"One other thing about him," Reagan began. "He's had a little bit of a rough life."

"What do you mean?" her mother asked.

"Well, he's spent a lot of his life with just his brother and father."

"Oh no. His mother passed?" Barbara asked.

"No, she just walked out one day. He was only nine."

"Oh, that's terrible. Poor thing," her mom said.

"I know, it's awful. I don't know how he coped. It must have been so hard for him," Reagan said.

"He must be strong to be able to deal with something like that," her mother suggested.

"Yeah," Reagan said. She waited for a moment, not sure of what to say next.

"So, when do we get to meet this young man?" her dad asked.

"Hopefully soon," Reagan said. "I wanted us to get to know each other a little better first, and see what happens. This is all so new still."

"There's certainly nothing wrong with that. No need to rush things," Tim said.

"That's right. But we'll be happy to meet him whenever you're ready," Barbara added.

Reagan helped her mother prepare the rest of the meal. By early afternoon, they were sitting at the table, eating their Christmas dinner. There was entirely way too much ham, mashed potatoes, corn, gravy, and rolls for three people. Barbara seemed excited to have leftovers, though. She prepared several to-go containers for her daughter to take with her.

"Thanks, Mom. That'll be supper for me for two days," Reagan told her, while she packed the bowls into a bag.

"You're welcome, dear. You takin' off soon?"

"Yeah, I probably need to get out of here by three. I'm gonna visit for a little bit and help you clean up first."

"You don't have to do that, honey," Barbara insisted.

"I know, but I want to, please."

Tim took out the trash while Reagan helped her mother load the dishwasher. They enjoyed the precious time they got to spend together. Barbara initiated some girl-talk with her daughter about her early relationship with Jackson, something she had looked forward to for years. Reagan enjoyed the rare opportunity, but the afternoon with her parents was soon coming to an end. They each wrapped their daughter up in one last hug and helped her to her car.

"Thank you again for the money. I love you guys so much," Reagan said, as she climbed into the driver's seat.

"You're welcome, hon," her father told her.

"Keep in touch," her mother added.

"I will. And I'll let you know when I get there."

"You going to see Jackson tonight?" Barbara asked.

"Yeah, we're gonna eat dinner," Reagan said, smiling. "But we established a no-gift rule. That way, no one feels pressured to buy anything."

"That's probably good. It's still early, anyway. You have a lot to learn about each other," her mother told her.

"I hope so. Well, I better get going. You guys get inside out of the cold," Reagan said.

"We're going. Merry Christmas," her father replied.

"Love you," Barbara said.

"Love you guys. And Merry Christmas. I'll call you when I get there."

With a wave from each of them, Reagan pulled out onto the street and drove away.

∼

After a couple of agonizing highway hours, Reagan parked her car at her apartment building, back in Newbrook. She called her mother, as promised, then immediately called Jackson to let him know she was home. They had planned to eat dinner and enjoy a relaxing evening. He let her know that he would be there around six to get her, giving her plenty of time to get ready.

Reagan glanced out the window when she heard Jackson's Camaro pull up outside. She smiled, watching him climb out of his car. He looked handsome, as usual, but tonight he was especially breath-taking. It was moments like this that made her wonder if it was all a dream. Seconds later, he knocked on the door, and she didn't hesitate to open it.

"Merry Christmas," he told her immediately.

She blushed and did her best to reply. "Merry Christmas," she said softly.

"Wow. You look great," Jackson said.

"Thank you. So do you," she replied. Reagan had slipped on the only nice dress she had for the occasion, hoping she would at least look comparable to him. "Um, you can come in if you want. Or I'm ready, if you just wanna go."

"We can go, that's cool," he replied.

"Okay."

They were traveling to one of the only open restaurants in town. There wasn't a dress code, but it was still considered a nice establishment for dinner by most of the locals. Reagan and Jackson felt lucky and grateful that they were able to go on Christmas evening. When they pulled into the full parking lot, Jackson circled the building a few times, waiting for an open spot.

"I can't believe this many people go out on Christmas Day," Reagan said.

"Me either," Jackson agreed.

"I can't say I blame them, though. It's a lot of work to cook a big meal," she added.

He nodded. "Yeah, that's true."

"You should have seen all the food my mom made today," she told him.

"Oh yeah? I bet it was good," he replied.

"It was. She sent a bunch home with me. You can have some, if you want it."

"I might take you up on that. But right now, I'm just hoping we can eat here," Jackson told her.

"I know, I'm starting to get a little worried," Reagan replied. Right on cue, a couple walked out of the restaurant and headed across the parking lot to their car. "Ooo, right there. I think they're leaving," she said, pointing.

Jackson pulled up slowly and waited for them to back out, so he could have the parking spot. Their patience paid off and, soon enough, they were walking inside. He opened the wooden door for Reagan. The buzzing noise of the crowd within immediately vibrated both of their eardrums. They weaved in and out of people, trying to reach the hostess at the podium.

"Two tonight?" the girl asked them.

"Yes," Jackson told her. "I have a reservation."

"What's the name?" she asked.

"Holloway."

She took a moment to check the book, then grabbed two menus and handed them to the blonde girl next to her. "Reservation for Holloway."

The blonde smiled at Jackson and Reagan, then motioned them to follow. "Right this way." She led them down a pathway toward a room in the back. "It's a good thing you guys made a reservation. I'm pretty sure the whole town is here tonight."

"Looks like it," Jackson replied.

"Don't worry, it's a little quieter back here."

"Thank you," Reagan said.

"You're welcome," the girl replied. She led them through double doors. "Here you go," she said, directing them to their reserved table. "Your waitress will be right with you."

"Thanks," Jackson said.

"No problem."

The girl walked away, and they sat down at the small table made for two, one across from the other. Only a few other couples sat in the room, and it was much quieter, as she had said. The lighting was fairly dim, a soft cloth was draped over the edges of the table, and a small candle burned in the middle.

"This is really beautiful," Reagan said. She struggled to contain her excitement as she looked at the menu.

"Yeah, it looks great," Jackson replied.

They examined the menu together in the flickering glow. Other than the faint hum from the crowd outside the doors, all they could hear was whispering from the handful of people in the room and soft music coming through the speakers. After a few minutes passed, their waitress walked in with a tray of drinks for the other tables. She distributed the beverages, then made her way over to them.

"Sorry about your wait. My name is Deb. Can I get your drinks?"

"Go ahead," Jackson said, looking at Reagan.

"Oh, uh, I think I'll try the raspberry lemonade, please."

"And for you, sir?" the waitress asked.

"Coke, please," he told her.

"I'll have those right out."

Reagan resumed reading the menu. Jackson had already set his off to the side and was watching Reagan. She knew what she would like to have, but it turned her stomach a little when she saw the price. She looked at some of the other options, then her eyes went back to that plate of seafood. The fingers on her right hand began tapping the table, while her left hand rested on her temple.

"Reagan," Jackson said.

"Yeah?" she asked.

"You get whatever you want," he told her. "It's okay."

She pulled her left hand down. Her gaze left the menu and looked up at his face. "But . . . I don't know . . ."

"It's okay," he said again.

"Are you sure? It's expensive." Her voice quivered.

"Please. I want you to get whatever you want. I promise it's okay."

Reagan blushed as he flashed an irresistible grin at her. "Thank you," she finally said.

The waitress returned shortly with their drinks. "Coke for you." She sat Jackson's glass down. "And a raspberry lemonade. Are you ready to order?" she asked them.

Reagan looked at Jackson, silently trying to confirm that he was ready, too.

"Go for it," he told her.

"Okay. I'll take the crab legs," Reagan started.

"What two sides would you like?" the waitress asked.

"A baked potato and green beans, please."

Jackson grimaced at first, then switched to a straight face. Reagan immediately noticed his awkward expression. She chuckled. "Oh, I forgot to tell you. I love green beans."

He started laughing and the waitress grinned hesitantly. "Um . . . what can I get you, sir? Green beans?" she asked.

"Nah, I'm good. I'll have the New York strip, please. With, uh, mashed potatoes and corn.

"How would you like your steak cooked?"

"Medium's fine. Thank you," he said.

"We'll have that right out."

Reagan and Jackson enjoyed the delicious food and each other's company, until the restaurant began to grow quiet. They eventually decided it was time to go, bundling up in their winter gear. Jackson walked by her side, hand-in-hand, until they reached the car.

They rolled out onto the vacant street and traveled back to Reagan's apartment. She quietly looked out the window at the lights, as they passed the old houses. It was hard for her to believe that Christmas Day had already come and was nearly over. When the tires of the car came to a stop across the street from her building, it took her a moment to realize that they were already there. She looked at her little tree, sitting in the window a couple of floors up.

"Thank you for dinner, Jackson," she said.

"You're welcome. I had a great time."

"Me too." Reagan smiled for a moment, then a somber expression replaced it.

"What's wrong?" Jackson asked.

"Nothing. I had a great time. I'm a little sad that it's over, I guess," she told him.

"Oh. Yeah, me too," he replied. He twiddled his thumbs for a moment, before asking her a question. "Hey, would you want to meet my dad tomorrow? He said he'd like to meet you."

Reagan nodded and answered almost immediately. "Yes, that would be great."

"All right. I can come pick you up, if you want," he offered.

"You can if you want to. Or . . . how about I just drive there? That way, you don't have to drive back and forth twice."

"Sure. That'll work. We live at the end of Cherry Street, in the cul-de-sac. It's the only brick house," he told her.

"Okay. I don't think I can screw that up," she replied. She looked up at her window again, tapping her thigh with her fingers. "Would . . . would you like to come up? Maybe watch a movie or something?"

He smiled and she proceeded to melt in her seat.

"Yeah, let's do it," he replied.

Reagan blushed and her eyes widened. "What . . . uh . . ."

"Oh, no. That's not what I meant," he nervously spluttered. "I meant, let's hang out . . . watch a movie . . . you know . . ."

She grinned at him. "It's okay, I know what you meant."

He started laughing, then apologized.

"Come on, I'll let you pick the movie," Reagan said.

CHAPTER 9

The following day, Reagan spent the morning preparing herself to meet Jackson's father. She was far more nervous than she wanted to be and didn't even understand why. Her meager experience with this type of situation was creating a flood of emotions and thoughts. *What if he thinks I'm weird? What if he's expecting someone . . . not like me?* Reagan drove herself to near madness before finally getting dressed to leave. She fixed her hair, put on her coat, clutched her purse, then headed out the door.

She didn't have far to drive to get there. About twelve blocks and three stoplights later, she rolled into the cul-de-sac at the end of Cherry Street. Jackson wasn't kidding. His house was the only brick home around. It was a ranch-style abode, with beautiful shutters. Two leafless maple trees stood in the front yard and the pathway to the door ran between them.

Reagan parked behind Jackson's Camaro and shut her car off. The short hike up the sidewalk seemed more like a mile, especially in the twenty-one-degree weather. She reached the door and stopped on the welcome mat. One deep, nervous breath later, she knocked. It only took a few moments before Jackson opened it.

"Hey, I see you found it," he said.

"No problem," she replied.

"Come in," he said. She followed his lead and waited for him to shut the door. "Here, I'll take your coat."

"Thanks," she said.

Jackson hung up her coat in the closet behind him, then turned back to Reagan. "Hope you're hungry. Dad's grilling some burgers."

"Sounds great," Reagan replied.

"I think he might actually be the only crazy person that grills in December," Jackson said.

Reagan smiled. "Well, I like it. It gives you a taste of summer when you need it most."

Right on cue, the sliding door to the back patio opened. A bundled-up man shuffled through the door, then closed it immediately.

"Oh, good lord, it's cold out," Jackson's father grumbled. He took off his gloves and hat and continued talking, having not yet looked up. "These burgers are gonna be g . . ." He stopped, finally noticing that their guest had arrived. A smile stretched across his face, then he stepped toward her. "Hello. You must be Reagan."

"Reagan? Who's Reagan?" she said, as straight-faced as she could.

Jackson looked down at her, surprised at the humor she had rarely shown in his presence. His father's smile disappeared, replaced with a look of confusion.

"Uh . . . um . . ." he began to stutter.

She grinned a little and decided to set things straight. "I'm sorry, this is why I'm not a comedian. Yes, I'm Reagan. It's so good to meet you."

His father busted up laughing. "Now, that's funny. I like that. David . . . nice to meet you." He reached out and shook her hand. "So, Reagan, are you hungry? You like burgers?"

"Yes, and yes. It sounds great. And smells great, I might add," she said.

"Well, thank you. Would you like cheese on yours?"

"Sure, thanks."

David walked to the fridge to get the cheese slices, then headed back outside. Jackson turned to Reagan and chuckled.

"I didn't know you had a prankster side to you. That was cute."

"I didn't either. I've spent most of my life afraid to speak. I figured it was a good time to open up a little," she said.

"Come on, I'll show you around." He took her hand and led her around the house, eventually stopping at the end of a hallway. "And this is my room," he finished.

Reagan stepped into the tidy bedroom. "Very nice," she told him. "Makes mine look pathetic."

"Well, I tidied it up a little. I'll admit, it's not usually this nice," Jackson said, shrugging his shoulders.

"Damn right, it's not," David said, appearing behind them.

Jackson turned and looked at his dad, who was standing in the doorway. "Thanks, dad."

Reagan started laughing.

"See? She thinks I'm funny," David said. "Food's ready when you guys are."

"Alright, we're comin'," Jackson said.

They walked back to the kitchen to find a mini buffet set up on the island. Buns, condiments, chips, pickles, and a plate of hamburgers sat in a row, with a stack of paper plates at the end. "It might not be summer, but we can pretend it is, don't you think?" David asked.

"Definitely," Reagan answered.

"Go ahead, Reagan. Jump in there," David insisted.

He didn't have to tell her twice. She reached for a plate and made a sandwich, while the other two followed behind her. They took a seat at the table, then David jumped back up and made his way to the refrigerator.

"I'm sorry, Reagan, I forgot to ask. Would you like a Coke? Water? Let me see what else we got here . . ." he continued as he searched the shelves.

"A Coke is great. Thank you," she replied.

David carefully held onto three cans and made his way back to the table. "Here you go. So, Reagan, tell me a little about yourself."

"Oh," she mumbled, covering her mouth full of food. She motioned with her index finger for him to give her a second, then swallowed her last bite. "Sorry. This is very good, by the way."

"Thank you," he replied.

"Let's see, about me. So, I'm afraid I'm not all that exciting, to be honest with you. I work at the mall at Katie's, for now anyway. I like to read and watch movies. I'm from Morgan, a small town about two hours from here. And I was an only child. So, it was just me and mom and dad until I went to college."

"Oh, yeah? What did you go for?" David asked.

"Well, I was an art major at first, then I started taking classes for business, too," she told him.

"Her paintings are great, dad," Jackson bragged. "She's gonna sell them one day."

"Well, that's the hope, anyway," she added. "Just savin' up right now."

"Hey, now that's cool. You don't hear that every day," David said. "I'd like to see 'em sometime. And I'll definitely buy one," he added. "Sounds like you're very smart and creative."

"That's very nice of you to say. I don't feel like it right now, but I'll get everything sorted out eventually."

"You got plenty of time. And there's nothing wrong with trying to save a little money first. Nothin' wrong with that at all," David told her. He took a bite, quickly chewing and swallowing it. "By the way, Reagan, I hope you had a Merry Christmas."

"I did, thanks. Same to you."

"We did. We didn't do a whole lot, so that was nice. Dallas was here for a little while, then he went to see his girlfriend."

"Ah, okay. Is he home on break?" she asked.

"Yeah. Well, sort of. He isn't here much. He's out runnin' around somewhere. Can't keep that boy still," David said. "Jackson's always on the move, too, but not quite as bad as Dallas."

Jackson continued to eat as if his name hadn't been mentioned.

"I noticed," Reagan said, glancing at him as she took a swig of her drink.

"So, what are ya doin' for New Year's, Reagan?" David asked.

"Uh, I don't know, actually," she said slowly, unsure of how to answer the question. She and Jackson hadn't discussed the subject yet.

"Well, if you kids don't have any plans, you're more than welcome to hang out with me for the evening. I don't know how long I'll stay awake, but I'll try."

Reagan smiled and looked at Jackson. "I'd love to come over . . . unless . . . I didn't know what you wanted to do," she stammered.

"Sure," Jackson agreed. "I hadn't really thought about it yet, but I'm fine with that, if you are."

"Great. You like chili, Reagan?" David asked.

"I love it," she answered.

"Good. I'll make a batch of my famous chili. I don't know if Jackson told you or not, but my chili is pretty darn good. Just be careful; once you try it, you'll be addicted."

Jackson nodded. "It's true."

"He did. He said it's his favorite food, actually," she reassured him.

David held his hand out. "See, that's what I mean."

Reagan finished eating with Jackson and his father, then stayed a few hours to hang out. She had no reason to rush out, but she eventually decided to head back, to keep from imposing on another meal.

"Well, I think I'm gonna head home," she told them.

"You sure? You can stay for supper if you want," David said.

"Oh, I appreciate the offer. But I better get some laundry done before work tomorrow. Might paint a little. Thank you so much, though," she replied.

"You're welcome over any time you want," he said.

"Hey, I'll see you Friday, right?" she reminded him.

"I'll have the chili waiting."

Jackson stood up and walked with Reagan over to the door. He took her coat back out of the closet and handed it to her. They stepped out into the cold air and Jackson strolled next to her along the sidewalk. "Sorry if dad seemed a little clingy. He doesn't get much company, as I'm sure you could tell."

"He was no trouble at all. I'm just glad he talked to me," she said.

"He really liked you," Jackson said.

"You think so?"

"Yes. I know he did."

"Wow. That's good, huh? I thought I blew it with that terrible joke," Reagan said.

"No way. If anything, that might have been the moment he knew."

"Knew what?"

"That you're perfect," he finished.

She stopped in her tracks, nearly to her car, and turned to face him. "I don't understand."

"Understand what?"

"Why you like me," she said.

Jackson grinned, shivering from head to toe. He looked away for a moment, as if trying to plan his next words. Then he gazed back at her. "Because you're everything I'm not."

Reagan looked back at him. She didn't know whether to cry

or laugh. The mixed emotions expressed on her face must have confused for him.

"What? Did I say something wrong?"

"No, that was very sweet. It's just kind of funny that you said it," she told him.

"Why?"

"'Cause I said the same thing about you to Donna. I told her that you're everything I'm not."

"You did?" he asked.

"Yes, I swear."

"Well, then I guess we're meant to be," he said. He kissed her as well as he could with shaking legs.

She kissed him back, then pulled away. "You need to get inside before you get sick."

He smiled. "Be careful going home."

"I will," she said as she climbed into the driver's seat.

He waved and ran back to the house.

The following week was filled with complaints from the terrible trio at work, Jen's excitement over Reagan's new relationship, and a swarm of post-Christmas gift returns. Reagan took it one day at a time, waiting patiently for Friday. When it finally arrived, she found herself watching the clock, from the time she punched in until it was time to leave. She gave Jen a quick 'goodbye', then hurried to her car.

After a brief stop at the store for supplies, she arrived at home and started preparing cupcakes. The oven wouldn't bake them as fast as she wished it would, but she was getting dressed and ready to leave before she knew it. Tupperware in hand, she started up the car, which had hardly had a chance to cool back down.

Reagan hadn't made plans for New Year's Eve in several years, at least none beyond the comfort of her couch. And even though it made her feel silly, she had picked up some noise-makers and colorful headgear for the occasion. She started her drive to Cherry Street, feeling excited enough to hop out and run the rest of the way if she had to. Once again, she parked her car behind Jackson's and made her way up the sidewalk. Jackson opened the door before her feet could get there.

"Come on. Come on. Dad's driving me nuts, wanting to know where you're at," he told her.

"I got ready as fast as I could," she replied.

"What's this?" he asked, looking at the Tupperware.

"Oh, a little surprise." She cracked the lid just enough to allow him to see the icing and smell the chocolate. Reagan smiled at him, waiting on his reaction.

He was speechless at first, but his expression spoke for itself. Like a kid in a candy store, the cupcakes seemed to excite him.

"Wow, those look amazing," he told her. "You didn't have to do that."

"It wasn't a problem at all. Actually, I used boxed mix and it required very little effort."

"Hell, that doesn't matter. Thank you. Dad will have a cow. Chocolate is his favorite," he told her.

"Good. That's even better," she said as she snapped the lid shut.

They walked toward the kitchen, where Jackson's father was standing at the stove, stirring the contents of a two-gallon pot. David turned his head in time to catch them entering the doorway.

"Reagan! You made it," he said. He left the spoon in the pot and stepped over to chat with the guest. "You ready to enjoy some tasty chili?" he asked her.

"Yes, it smells great. And I'm starving," she said. "Um, this is for you," she added, as she handed the container of cupcakes to David.

He smiled, looked at Jackson, then looked back at Reagan. "You didn't have to bring anything." He opened the lid, examined the delicious, fluffy, palm-sized desserts, then reached out and hugged her. "That was very thoughtful of you, Reagan. Thank you."

"You're very welcome, but I promise it was no trouble."

"All right, all this food is making me hungry. Let's eat," David declared. "Reagan, you go first."

"Okay, thanks," she replied.

"There's some cheese and onion over here, if you'd like some. Oh, and most importantly, the bread and peanut butter," he told her.

"You do that, too? I love peanut butter bread with chili," she told him.

"It's the best," he replied.

They each got their chili, peanut butter sandwich, and a cupcake and sat in the living room to eat and watch TV. Reagan had sprinkled cheese and onion in her bowl, willing to risk the heartburn that she would most certainly suffer afterward. But when she took the first bite, she knew it would be worth it.

"Oh, wow. I get why this is your favorite," she said to Jackson.

"Good, isn't it?" Jackson asked.

"Yes. Very good. Mr. Holloway, this is great. Thanks again for making it."

"You're welcome. And please, call me David." He flipped the channels, unsure of what to watch. "Would you guys rather watch football or . . . a movie? Those are about the only reasonable options for the time being."

"Anything is fine with me," she replied.

"All right, well, this is good, I guess," he said, settling on a game. He took a bite of chili, then continued talking. "I gotta be honest, guys. I don't know if I'll make it to midnight. It was a long week."

"Oh, gosh. Now I feel even more terrible that you took the time to cook," Reagan said.

"I promise, it's quite all right. This was a break compared to the week we had, huh?" he said, looking at Jackson.

Jackson nodded, too engaged with his chili to answer out loud.

"That's right. Jackson said you guys were working in an office building or something," she said.

"Yup. We were there all week. It's just tedious work, that's all," David told her.

"I can only imagine. It has to be hard. I don't know how you guys do it," she said.

"Well, you get used to it after a while. And I don't do a lot of the back-breaking work anymore. The guys do most of that."

"Ha," Jackson finally spoke, squeezing the words in between bites. "He's just being modest. Dad does a lot for the guy that owns the company. He makes most of us look bad," Jackson insisted.

"Oh, yeah?" Reagan asked.

David looked as if he was going to disagree with his son's statement, but Jackson continued before he could get a word in.

"Yes. I swear, he could break his arm and he would keep working." Jackson said.

David gave up and tossed his right hand in the air.

"That's okay," Reagan said. "He's a hard worker."

"Thank you," David said.

"Yeah, it'll be alright 'til he overdoes it one day," Jackson said.

"Oh, please," David started. "You act like I'm eighty years old. I'm only fifty. I got a lot of work ahead of me still."

"That's right. You're fifty, not twenty, dad. And why do you have a lot of work ahead of you? That's why you own the company, so others can do the work."

"Yes, and no. I can't do that. I'm not built that way. You'll understand one day," David argued.

Reagan sat on the couch next to Jackson, listening to the guys argue while they scarfed down their chili. She didn't know if she should speak or just watch football. They finally paused long enough for her to change the subject.

"This is such a nice house," she said.

"Thank you. Built it myself," David told her.

"See what I mean? He never stops," Jackson said.

Reagan tried to control the urge to laugh, but she let it out anyway. The guys both looked at her in surprise. "S . . . sorry," she muttered between cackles. "You guys crack me up. You fight like an old married couple."

"It's no wonder. He's so stubborn," Jackson said.

"I'm stubborn?" David asked. "You're the stubborn one."

"Yeah, I wonder where I got it from," Jackson added.

"Okay, okay. Guys. Let's . . . let's . . ." She tried to think of something they could do or talk about that would stop them from arguing. *Could we play a game? No. Terrible idea. Come on, think of something.*

"Let's try these delicious cupcakes," David suggested.

Reagan nodded in approval. "Yes. Good idea, huh?" she asked Jackson, giving him a gentle nudge.

"Yeah, well, I ate mine already," he said quietly.

"You did?" she asked, having not even noticed.

"Yeah, I kinda squeezed it in between bites of chili."

"Oh," she replied, trying not to laugh. "Was it okay?"

"Hell, yeah. It was great," Jackson said.

"M'yeah . . ." David mumbled through a mouthful of cake. "Weally good."

"Charming, dad," Jackson said, staring at his father.

Reagan laughed, then decided to try her cupcake, too. She was surprised at how good they were. The chocolate chips she had added to the batter gave them extra pizazz.

The arguing stopped after the cupcake eating session and the three of them grew quiet, while they watched TV. Around eleven, David turned the channel to one of the stations covering the New Year's celebration. A random mix of musicians performed on stage, helping the time go faster for the last hour of the year. Jackson managed to eat three more cupcakes during the process of waiting for the ball to drop.

David made it to about eleven forty before he finally dozed off. His chin had dropped down to his chest. Jackson elbowed Reagan and nodded toward his father. She smiled at the sight of him.

"He almost made it."

"I'm shocked he made it that long, honestly." He wrapped her up in his left arm and she laid her head on his chest.

They sat together and watched the last few performances before the countdown began. Reagan's heart began to race as the timer on the bottom corner of the TV grew closer and closer to zero. She didn't know what to expect. Every New Year's celebration of her life, she had spent with her parents or alone.

Ten, nine, eight . . . the voices on TV shouted. For every second counted, her heart would beat twice. *Four, three, two, one* . . . *Happy New Year!* She smiled, cherishing the moment. Jackson reached his right hand across and placed it on her cheek. She looked up at him and swallowed the lump in her throat.

"Happy New Year," he told her.

"Happy New Year," she replied. He leaned in and kissed her for a moment, then pulled back and smiled. "Oh, I almost forgot," she said, getting up to grab the bag next to her shoes. "I brought these." She pulled the hats and noisemakers out of the bag.

He grinned as she stuck a blue hat on top of his head and handed him a noisemaker to match. She donned her celebration apparel and took a deep breath, then they gave the blowers all they could handle. The sudden spike in decibel level startled David for only a moment, then he went right back to sleep. Jackson laughed at his father's reaction, then curled back up with Reagan on the couch. They watched the ongoing celebration and colorful display of confetti on the screen. Outside, the sound of noisemakers and fireworks filled up the entire neighborhood. Reagan closed her eyes, taking in the sound.

∽

The following morning, David stood at the stove once again. A pan full of sizzling bacon sat next to a pan of scrambled eggs. The aroma of the smoked bacon was enough to awaken Reagan. She slowly opened her eyes, confused for a moment about where she was. Then she looked over at Jackson, who still held her in his left arm, then sat up and yawned.

"Jackson," she said. He remained unresponsive. "Jackson," she said a little louder, with a poke to his arm. He cracked an eyelid and looked at her. "Good morning," she said.

"Morning," he replied.

"You guys hungry?" David asked as he walked into the living room.

"Yes, it smells great," Reagan answered quickly. She grew a little nervous. "Uh, I'm sorry. I don't remember falling asleep."

David chuckled. "It's okay. You guys looked comfortable, so I just covered you up."

"Thank you. And thanks for cooking . . . again," she added.

"It's no trouble. I kinda like cookin', actually," he insisted.

Reagan enjoyed yet another meal at Jackson's house before deciding it was time to head home and take a shower. It saddened her a little that she had to leave. Not only did she want to stay with Jackson, but she also got the feeling that David enjoyed her company. She helped the men clean up the kitchen before eventually putting on her jacket and boots. Jackson went out to start her car for her.

"You know, you can come over anytime you want," David told her, as he handed her the empty Tupperware container. "Sorry, I think they're all gone."

"That's good. That's what they were for. Plus, I wouldn't have been able to eat all those, anyway."

Jackson came back in the door. "Damn, it's cold. I'd give it a minute to warm up." Jackson gave his dad a look, as if to ask for a few minutes alone.

"Well, I'm gonna go get a shower. Reagan, it's been a pleasure," David told her.

"Likewise," she replied.

"Be careful driving home," he said.

"Will do. Thanks again for having me. And for cooking all the delicious food."

"Anytime, dear. See ya next time," he finished as he walked away.

"Bye," she said. She turned to Jackson. "I had a lot of fun," she said.

"Me too." He paused for a minute. "You don't have to go yet, if you don't want."

"Well, I don't *want* to, but I do kinda want to get cleaned up and get some painting done," she told him.

"I understand."

"You want to come over later?" she asked.

"Yes . . . please," he said, laughing.

"Your dad is really cool. And he cares a lot about you. I can see it."

"I know. We just bicker sometimes, that's all," he said.

She laughed. "That's okay. How do you think I know how much he loves you?"

He nodded in return. "I'll see you later," he said.

"I'll be waitin' on ya," she replied, turning to walk out the door.

Once again, Reagan drove home in a daze. It was an amazing feeling to be held the way that he held her, and that was all she could think about. She didn't know what would happen from here on out. And she didn't know exactly what they were going to be. But she knew that this was one hell of a way to begin the new year.

CHAPTER 10

By the time mid-January rolled around, another eight inches of snow had fallen, and Reagan had finished yet another week of work at the store. She was feeling better than she had in a long time. The tremendous high she felt from the way Jackson respected her had changed her life more than she could have imagined. Even the dreadful time she spent at the mall, Monday through Friday, seemed a little brighter now that she had something to look forward to afterward.

Of course, she and Donna had a lot more to discuss, now that Reagan's life had changed direction. On this particular Saturday, Reagan noticed an exaggerated smile on Donna's face the moment she walked in the door. She approached the counter slowly, studying Donna's expression.

Then she finally asked, "Alright, what's going on?"

"Well, as a matter of fact, I have some news for you," Donna replied.

"Okay, I'm listening," Reagan said, with interest, as she leaned on the counter.

"Mary officially announced that she is retiring at the end of January."

"You're kidding!" Reagan shouted louder than she had anticipated. "Sorry," she whispered. "Really? That was fast."

"I know," Donna replied. "I knew it was coming, but I didn't realize it would be that soon."

"That's great! I guess I should go apply right now. Or should I just go talk to Vickie?" Reagan pondered.

"Actually, I already did. As soon as I heard the news, I told her that I thought you would be the perfect candidate," Donna said.

"What did she say?" Reagan asked, struggling to contain her excitement.

"She agreed," Donna answered, nearly before Reagan could ask. "She said she would love to have you here. Of course, she'll probably still have you apply, but I know she's gonna hire you, no matter what."

"Oh, that's so awesome." Reagan reached across the counter and tried her best to hug her friend. "Thank you. Thank you so much for recommending me. I really appreciate it."

"It's not a problem at all, dear. We can't wait to have you here."

"Is she here today?" Reagan asked.

"She will be for a little bit. She doesn't usually stay long on Saturdays, but I told her you'd probably be in," Donna replied.

Reagan paused a moment to let the news sink in. "Okay, I'm gonna go fill out the application. Then I'll find a book and I'll be back in a little bit." Reagan headed upstairs to Vickie's office. She found herself struggling to walk on shaky legs. It wasn't so much nervousness that was getting to her, but an overwhelming excitement. She wasn't sure if it was due to the idea of leaving Katie's, or because she was going to get paid to do what she loved, or maybe both. But she knew for sure that it couldn't happen soon enough.

When she arrived at the office, the door was open. Vickie, a small, middle-aged woman, was sitting at her desk, working on the computer. She looked up at the subtle sound coming from Reagan's jacket.

"Reagan, good morning. I was expecting you."

"Morning," Reagan replied. "You know me . . . every Saturday morning."

"Yes, you may be our most loyal visitor," Vickie said, chuckling.

"So, Donna told me that Mary's retiring."

"Yeah, she felt like it was time. Her husband retired five years ago. I'm sure she's ready to spend some time with him at home," Vickie said.

"I don't blame her at all." Reagan paused awkwardly for a moment, her touch-and-go social skills rearing their ugly head. "I thought, um, would it be all right if I apply for her position? I know it's early but . . ."

"We would love to have you, Reagan," Vickie said without hesitation.

"Really?"

"Of course. You're perfect for the position. You're smart, you're generous and likable, and you may know the library better than I do."

Reagan smiled. "Thank you."

"I'll have you complete the paperwork, mostly so I can have it on file. But, as long as you want the position, it's yours," Vickie reassured her.

"Yes, very much," Reagan said. "And I can walk here. I'll never have to worry about car trouble," she added.

Vickie laughed again. She picked up the paper that she already had ready on the corner of her desk and handed it to Reagan. "Go ahead and fill this out and bring it in whenever you have time, so I can get your information in the system."

"Oh, I'll do it now if that's okay. It won't take long," Reagan insisted.

"Sure, take your time."

Reagan completed the forms as quickly and neatly as she could and returned them to Vickie. "Here you go."

"Thank you. I will get in touch with you soon, so we can get your tax information, work schedule, and stuff like that all worked out."

"That sounds great. Thank you so much," Reagan told her again, before heading out the door.

She wandered to the fiction section to pick out a new book, then hurried to the front desk. Donna seemed to be waiting on her return, as she was already looking in the direction of Reagan's favorite aisle.

"Well, how did it go?" she asked .

"It went great. She had me fill out some paperwork, but she basically told me the job is mine," Reagan said.

"Yay! I'm so happy for you. And you certainly deserve it."

"Thanks, Donna. I can't wait. I have a feeling the next couple weeks are gonna drag."

"Probably. But it'll be over before you know it," Donna said, sliding the book back to Reagan. "You're good to go."

"All right. I guess I'll see you next Saturday," Reagan said.

"Have a good weekend. And congratulations, honey."

Reagan walked into her apartment and immediately called Jackson.

"Hey, what's up?" he asked.

"Guess what?" Reagan started, trying to contain her excitement.

"What?"

"I'm gonna work at the library."

"Hey, that's great, Reagan," he replied.

"I know, right? Donna told me, like a month ago, that she thought Mary was gonna retire, but we didn't realize it would be this soon. I can't even tell you how relieved I am. I mean, not that Mary's retiring. She's really sweet. I'm just relieved that I'm the one that gets to take her spot. I can't wait to get out of Katie's," Reagan told him.

"I don't blame you. I don't know how you work with those girls. I can't stand them for two minutes, let alone forty hours a week."

"Yeah, it sucks, and trust me, I only go because I need the paycheck. I do feel bad about leaving Jen, though," she said. "Now she'll be stuck there with them by herself."

"Well, my guess would be, she'll probably find another job, too. I'm sure she'll understand. It's all right. You deserve to have a job that you don't dread going to every day," he reassured her.

"I know she'll be happy for me. I just hope she can find something. Jobs haven't been great lately."

"I'm sure something will come up. I'll keep an eye out for her. You know that."

"I appreciate that. Well, anyway, it sounds like the pay will be about the same as what I get now, so that's good," Reagan told him.

"Yeah, definitely. So, when do you start?" he asked.

"Mary's last day is the twenty-ninth, so I'll probably start on the thirty-first, I guess. I'm not sure yet. Vickie said she'd be in touch soon, to get everything sorted out."

"That's awesome, hon. And just think . . . only two more weeks with the terrible trio," he added.

"Ha, no kidding."

On Monday, Reagan parked in her usual spot, unsure of whether to feel happy or sad about giving her two weeks' notice. The vast majority of her body was overwhelmed with joy, but she still felt terrible about leaving Jen. Angie was supposed to be at work that day, so it was the perfect opportunity to break the news. But, before anything else, she wanted Jen to know.

As usual, Jen was in the breakroom at her locker, when Reagan walked in. Jen took a swig of her coffee as she shoved her coat into her locker. When she closed the door, Reagan was standing there, waiting.

"Oh, hey," Jen said. "I see I'm not the only one that showed up for another crappy week."

Reagan laughed. "Good morning, Jen."

"Leh! This coffee tastes like ass," Jen announced. She looked back at Reagan, who was desperately trying to keep a straight face. "What's up?" Jen asked.

"What?" Reagan asked.

"What's up?" Jen repeated. "You look like something's wrong?"

"Well, no. There's really nothing wrong. I kinda have something I want to tell you," Reagan said.

"Okay . . ."

"Okay. Well, I went to the library on Saturday. You know, like I always do."

"Yeah?" Jen asked, waiting on Reagan to continue.

"And Donna, the lady at the front desk, told me that one of the librarians, Mary, is retiring at the end of January. So . . . I uh . . . I," Reagan stuttered.

"Did you get the job?" Jen asked, with interest.

"I . . . yes. Yeah, they told me I could have the job."

"Oh, thank god," Jen said.

"What?" Reagan asked, stunned by her response.

Jen started laughing. "No, I didn't mean it like that. Sorry. Oh, you're gonna kill me."

Reagan tipped her head in confusion. "I don't understand."

"Okay. Reagan, we've been here for over a year now. You've always had my back and, frankly, you're the only thing that makes this job bearable. I decided a while back that I wouldn't leave unless you had an opportunity to leave."

Reagan looked away, trying not to tear up. "So, you're telling me that you stayed here just for me?"

"I guess you could say that. But I did it, knowing how those girls treated you. And I knew you wouldn't stay long. I wanted to have your back whenever they gave you shit," Jen insisted.

"Well, now I feel terrible," Reagan said.

"Why?"

"'Cause, you were staying to have my back, and I went out and got a job. I was just gonna leave you here." The guilt sickened her, and her eyes welled up.

"No. Don't you do that. We both knew that you were gonna get out of here, one way or another. It was just a matter of time. There was never a guarantee that I was gonna go anywhere. I would have killed you if you would have stayed here for me, and you know it," Jen told her. "Please don't cry, and don't be mad at me. And please, please, please don't feel bad for getting the job at the library. You deserve to like your job."

"You know what? I would probably like it here, if it wasn't for them," Reagan said.

"Yeah, I agree. I thought it was gonna be a good gig when I applied. Then I met them." Jen cringed and shrugged her shoulders.

Reagan started laughing. She took a deep breath in, then let it out. "All right, I guess I better go talk to Angie. Is she here?"

"Yeah, she's in there," Jen said. "I'm gonna go out. See ya when you're done. Good luck."

"Thanks," Reagan replied. After Jen walked out, Reagan knocked on the door in the breakroom that led to Angie's office.

"Come in," Angie called from inside. Reagan stepped in and shut the door behind her. "Morning, Reagan."

"Good morning. Do you have a minute?" she asked nervously.

"Sure. What's up?" Angie asked.

Reagan sat down in the chair in the corner, resting her hands on her lap. "Um, I wanted to let you know that a job opened up at the library. They said they'd love to have me there and it's perfect for me."

Angie nodded in agreement. "Yes, it's very perfect for you, actually. So, you took it, I'm assuming?"

"Yes."

"That's great, Reagan. I don't want you to leave but, as a friend, I'm happy for you," Angie said.

"Thank you. So, you're not mad?"

Her boss chuckled a little. "No, of course not. I wouldn't be mad at you for taking a job that you could be happier with. That's a good thing."

"I know, but I feel bad about leaving you short-handed," Reagan said.

"We'll be fine, I promise. So, when do you start? Or should I ask how long I have you for?" Angie said, laughing.

"Well, I should find out for sure sometime in the next couple of days, but I think I'll start there on the thirty-first. So, I'll be here 'til next Friday."

"Alright. I appreciate you giving me a heads up. That helps me a lot," Angie said.

"You're welcome. I would have told you sooner, but I only just found out."

"It's okay." They both paused for a moment, before Angie continued. "If you ever need anything, don't hesitate to ask, okay? I'd be happy to help you out in any way."

"Thank you, I appreciate that," Reagan replied.

"It's no problem at all. You've been a great employee. You're always here and on time. You work hard and you never complain. It's gonna be hard to replace you, I'll tell you that," Angie said, smiling.

Reagan smiled back at her. "Thanks, Angie. So, I guess I better get out there and help Jen."

"You bet. Get your butt out there," Angie joked.

Reagan walked out into the store. Jen was anxiously waiting on her at the counter.

"So how did it go?" Jen asked immediately.

"It went well. She was actually really happy for me."

"I figured she would be. If anything, she's probably bummed that she's losing such a good employee," Jen said.

"That's what she told me. But she said it would be all right." Reagan exhaled slowly. "I'm glad that's over. Now I can get through the next couple of weeks. But what about you?" she asked, turning to Jen. "What are you gonna do?"

"Uh, I think I'm gonna wait until she hires somebody, then I'll call my aunt Cindy and see if I can work in her store downtown. She owns that cool antique place on Main Street."

"Oh really? I've never been in there, but I've always wanted to check it out," Reagan told her.

"Well, if it all works out, I'll be there soon, and you can come see me," Jen suggested.

"Definitely," Reagan replied.

Reagan's final days went faster than she had anticipated. Before she knew it, she was saying "bye" to Angie for the last time. Of course, she reminded Jen that she would be in touch. And, naturally, she didn't even give the trio a final glance, let alone any words. She drove straight home, smiling brightly and feeling relieved at the freedom she felt.

Jackson had called Reagan before work that morning and told her he wanted to surprise her with something special on her last day. She had no idea what he had in mind, but she knew her car couldn't get her there fast enough. When she arrived, his car was already parked in the spot next to where she parked hers. He flashed a smile at her through the window, warming her even in the arctic-like temperature. She rushed out of the car to stand before him.

"All right, what're you up to?" she asked.

"Oh, nothin'," he replied.

"What's in the bag?" she asked, looking at the seat.

"Funny you should ask." He reached over to the passenger side and grabbed the grocery bag. "I picked up some supplies."

"Okay . . ." she replied, peeking in the bag.

"I'm gonna try to make you some lasagna," he said.

"You are? That sounds amazing."

"God, I hope so. And don't worry, I won't leave a mess or anything," he promised.

"Oh, it's okay. I'm not worried about that. But I don't know if I can sit and do nothing."

He closed the car door and they headed inside. "Please, I want to do this. You're just gonna have to find something else to do."

"Okay, fine. I'll paint or something. But if you want an extra hand at all, please tell me. Don't be stubborn," she said.

"Me? Stubborn?"

"Yes, you," she stressed.

He started laughing as he unloaded the supplies on the kitchen counter. "I even got us some . . ." he started, reaching into the bag for the last item. ". . . garlic bread."

"Mmm. I love it."

Reagan turned on the TV, trying to ignore the fact that Jackson was in the kitchen by himself, whipping up her celebration dinner. She paced around for the first fifteen minutes, alternating her gaze between the evening news and the handsome man in front of her stove. He glanced over at her and busted up laughing.

"Reagan, I'm fine. I promise. You don't need to help me," he insisted.

She smiled, not realizing how much she had been staring at him. "Sorry. I know you're fine. It just bothers me that you're working and I'm not helping, that's all."

"I appreciate it, but I want to do this. Relax, please."

"All right."

She stood for a moment, knowing that she had no interest in watching the news. So, she decided to turn it to a movie and place a fresh piece of canvas on the easel. Once she started with the brush, her concern for whether Jackson needed help with supper started to diminish. Before she knew it, a gorgeous bouquet of spring flowers had taken form on the canvas and the apartment had filled with the scent of parmesan and garlic.

"That's beautiful," Jackson told her as he looked over her shoulder.

She whipped around, surprised by his sudden presence. "Thank you."

"I mean it. I don't know how you do it. You truly have a gift," he said.

Reagan blushed a little. She wasn't used to other people seeing her artwork. "Thanks. I don't know how to explain it. I can see a picture, you know, in my mind. I can see it like it's right in front of me. Then I just transfer it to the canvas. I've always loved it. Even as a little girl, something about painting relaxed me."

"Well, I think it's amazing. I'm a little envious, to be honest with you," he said.

"Envious of me?" she asked.

"Yeah, you. You have a God-given talent that most people spend their life dreaming they could have. It's amazing and beautiful."

Reagan sat in silence for a moment, taking in the sincerity of his expression. She still didn't know how to read him at times, but this look was unmistakable. A great sense of happiness filled every inch of her body. She looked down at her toes, unable to hold his gaze.

"What's wrong?" he asked.

"Nothing's wrong. It just . . . it still surprises me sometimes that you're so nice to me," she said.

"Well, I lo . . ." he started.

Her heart seemed to skip a beat, and she suddenly grew nervous. No matter how much she wanted to speak, her larynx wouldn't produce any words. She looked back at him, waiting for him to make the next move.

"I love you," he finally said.

As hard as she tried to stop it, a teardrop rolled down her cheek. He reached up and wiped it away.

She took a deep, quivering breath then replied, "I love you, too."

He leaned in and kissed her, holding her close for what would indisputably be one of the best moments of her life.

Jackson pulled back finally, looked her in the eye, then asked, "Now, are you ready to eat?"

CHAPTER 11

W hether it was from Jackson's professed love or the new job at the library, Reagan found herself feeling like a different woman. She felt confident and energetic, perhaps for the first time in her life. And for once, she wasn't completely dreading Valentine's Day. In fact, the idea of having another reason to focus on their relationship was rather intriguing.

Jackson had, of course, made plans the weekend prior, for the couple to enjoy dinner together. He insisted that Reagan get all the seafood she desired. She had acknowledged the fact that he got pleasure out of trying to spoil her, though it was still difficult for her to accept all his acts of kindness. In addition to their evening out, Reagan told Jackson that there was one other thing that she would like to do. That being, as long as he was up for a little road trip.

"So, where we goin'?" he asked, as they headed down the highway.

"Well, I would say it's a surprise, but I really only have one place to go," she replied.

He nodded, seeming to understand what she had in mind. "All right, you think they'll like me?"

"Like you? They'll probably think it's a joke."

"Ha! Why would they think that?" he asked.

"'Cause I've never brought any guys home. It's definitely gonna be new for them. Plus, look at you," she said, gesturing at his attire.

He looked at his shirt and jeans, then back at her. "What? What's wrong?"

"Nothing's wrong. You look great."

"Well, thanks. But I don't understand why that would have anything to do with it."

"I'm just sayin', that's all," she said.

"You think your parents are gonna think that I'm . . . that I'm . . ."

"They won't think anything bad. They'll be impressed," she said.

He smiled. "You think so?"

"Uh, yeah. No question."

"Well, I was worried that I might not be what they wanted for their daughter," he said.

"Why would you say that? You're perfect."

"First of all, I'm far from it. And second, we've gone over this time and time again. If anyone is the lucky one, it's me. You're an amazing woman, and I guarantee they know it. I'm just some random guy," he said.

"No, you aren't," she told him. "You are what every woman dreams of having." He started laughing and shook his head. "What?" she said, laughing back at him. "You don't believe me?"

"No, I don't," he replied. "You couldn't pick me out of a crowd."

"All right. So, tell me why Valerie tried so hard to get your attention?" Reagan asked.

He shrugged his shoulders. "Your guess is as good as mine. 'Cause, she's desperate for attention?" he suggested.

"Well, yeah, but that's not the only reason. When you and your friends walked in, she picked you. She completely ignored them and picked you. What's that tell ya?" Reagan asked.

"Heck, I don't know. I did everything I could to ignore her without being mean."

Reagan smirked, remembering that day. "I know, it was hilarious. But she tried, anyway, because she saw the same thing in you that I see. And my parents will, too. Trust me," she reassured him.

"Thank you," he said, taking her hand.

Reagan had made this drive many times, but it certainly seemed much faster with Jackson by her side. She felt as if they had just left when they turned onto her parents' street.

"This is it here," she said, pointing at the next driveway.

Jackson pulled in and shut off the Camaro. He took a nervous breath. "All right."

"They're gonna love you. Come on." Reagan nudged him, excited to get inside.

He held her hand as they made their way toward the door. "So, this is where you grew up, huh?"

"Yup. My parents have lived here since they got married," she replied.

"Cool. Now I get to see some pictures of you," he said.

"Pictures of me?"

"Yeah. You know, as a kid and stuff."

"Oh, no, no, no. You don't want to do that," she assured him, as she knocked on the door.

"Ha, why not? I bet you were ador . . ." He trailed off as the door opened.

Barbara smiled back at them, her excitement obvious to the world. "You made it! Oh, come in. Come in. Reagan, honey, you didn't have to knock."

"I didn't wanna just walk in, mom," she said.

"It's okay, dear. Tim, they're here!" Barbara yelled down the hall.

Reagan looked up at Jackson, who smiled bashfully. She

attempted to convey her sympathy with a glance. As always, he seemed cool and collected. She, on the other hand, felt like her heart was going to leap out of her chest. After the longest twenty seconds she could imagine, her father made his way into the room.

"Sorry about that," Tim said, standing next to Barbara.

Reagan and her parents exchanged glances for a moment. None of them appeared to know who should speak next.

Her mother tried to help push it along. "So, Reagan . . ."

"Oh, right. Well, I'm sure you guys figured it out, but this is Jackson. Jackson, this is mom and dad," she said.

Jackson and Tim simultaneously reached out to shake hands. "Nice to meet you, sir," Jackson said.

"Nice to meet you, too. Call me Tim."

"Barbara," her mother said, proceeding to exchange her handshake with him.

"Nice to meet you," Jackson replied.

"Here, I can take your coats," Barbara offered.

Reagan and Jackson each handed their jacket over and Barbara hung them up next to the door.

"So, Jackson, Reagan told us you work in construction," Tim started.

"Yes. My dad owns his own business. I've been working for him for a few years now," Jackson replied.

"That's great. And that's a tough job, too," Tim said.

"Yes, sir."

"Is there any particular work that his company specializes in?" Tim asked with interest.

"Well, no, not really. We complete big projects sometimes in office buildings or for businesses. And sometimes we work on smaller residential jobs, like renovations and stuff. It changes week to week," Jackson told him.

"That sounds interesting. I bet it never gets boring either," Tim added.

"No, it's definitely not boring."

Barbara let the boys finish their conversation before speaking. "Are you guys hungry? Jackson, do you like tacos? I have some taco meat ready, if you'd like some."

"Yes, it smells great. I'd love some," he answered politely.

"Thanks, mom. You didn't have to do that," Reagan told her.

"Oh, it's alright, dear. I don't mind. Jackson, make yourself at home. You're welcome to anything you'd like," Barbara told him.

"Thank you," he said. Jackson and Reagan slipped off their shoes and made their way to the kitchen to find a taco buffet arranged on the counter. Tortillas, meat, and toppings were lined up in a row.

"Jackson, we have some pop in the fridge, if you'd like one. Or we have water or milk," she said.

"Thank you," he said. "It all looks great."

After they made their plates, Reagan gestured him toward the living room. "Mom, is it all right if we eat in here?"

"Sure, honey. That's all right. You guys watch whatever you want. The remote's probably on your dad's chair."

Reagan and Jackson sat on the couch, not wasting any time on trying their food.

"Mis is goo," Jackson mumbled.

"What?" she asked, laughing.

He swallowed his bite, then tried again. "This is good. Sorry."

"It is. I haven't had tacos in a long time," she said.

Jackson ate in silence for a minute as he looked around the living room. It didn't take him long to find what he was searching for.

"Aww, is that you?" he asked, looking at the eight by ten on the wall.

Her expression of disgust spoke for itself. "Yeah . . . yeah that's me," she muttered.

"What's wrong?" he asked her, chuckling at the look on her face. "I think it's adorable."

"I have a few words for it. Adorable isn't one of them," she said.

"Oh, come on. It's cute. What were you, like ten?"

"Wasn't she cute? She was in the fourth grade there," Barbara informed him as she entered the room. "The sweetest little girl you could possibly imagine. We never had any troubles with her. She always did her schoolwork and behaved so well."

"Well, I suppose that's because she was raised by good parents," Jackson said.

"Isn't that sweet of you. Thank you," Barbara replied. "I've got lots of pictures, if you want to see them."

Reagan nearly choked on her bite of food, attempting to tell her mother no, but Jackson intervened before she had a chance.

"I'd love to," he declared.

"Oh, wonderful! I'll be right back." Barbara set her plate down and hurried down the hallway.

Reagan glared at Jackson and Tim immediately started laughing.

"Now you've done it," he told Jackson. "She'll have you occupied for hours."

"That's all right. This is a rare opportunity for me," Jackson said.

"I'll get you back," Reagan warned. "You watch. The next time we see your dad, I'm gonna look at all your pictures. Of course, I'm sure all of yours are amazing so you won't mind anyway."

"Ha, good luck getting dad to get them out," he told her. "He's had 'em put away for a while."

Reagan instantly felt terrible. She hadn't even thought about the fact that childhood memories were probably different for him. Tim took a bite of his taco, looking back and forth between his daughter and Jackson. The room filled with awkwardness. Right on cue, Barbara reentered the room with a couple of large books, for which Reagan was actually thankful.

"Here we go, Jackson," Barbara said.

Reagan watched as her mother unveiled her entire childhood to Jackson. As embarrassing as it was for her, it was still better than the alternative of having no one to share the photos with. The joy he seemed to be getting from the experience made it all that much better. The afternoon clock ticked by rapidly and the time for visiting was coming to an end. Being Sunday, both of them were hoping to get home in time to relax for what was left of their precious time off.

"Well, you guys, we better get going. We gotta work tomorrow," Reagan finally told her parents.

"Oh, that's right, dear. I completely forgot to ask you how your new job is going," her mother said.

"It's great. So much better than being at the store every day, with the nightmares I had to work with."

"That's so good to hear. I'm glad you found something that's more enjoyable for you," Barbara said.

"Yeah, it's pretty much the perfect job, actually. And I don't dread going to work in the morning. I'm thinkin' I can keep saving up for another year or so, then I should be ready to open the store."

"Oh, that's so exciting," said her mom as she hugged her. She then turned to Jackson. "Well, Jackson, it was a pleasure meeting you. You are welcome back any time you'd like."

"Thank you. And thanks for having me and making the great food." He turned to face Tim and shook his hand. "It was nice meeting you."

"You, too, Jackson. Come back any time," Tim said.

"We will," Jackson promised.

After a couple of final hugs and "goodbyes", the pair walked out the door.

Jackson glanced at Reagan as they turned onto the highway. "Your parents are amazing."

"Aren't they? They've always been so loving and supportive, too. I'm truly blessed to have them," she said.

"And I loved the pictures of you. They were sweet. I don't know what you were so worried about," he added.

"I don't know. You know me, always self-conscious."

"I get it, but you don't need to be."

"Hey, I'm so sorry I mentioned your pictures, by the way. I wasn't thinking," she told him.

"That's all right. It's no big deal. And, you know, dad might get some of them out sometime, who knows."

"Only if he's comfortable with it. I don't want anything to be awkward for him," Reagan said.

"He'll be okay."

"And . . . I want you to be okay with it," she added.

"For you, I'll be all right," he replied, smiling.

She nodded, having no more words on the topic. Instead, she changed the subject. "I'm actually kind of excited for work tomorrow."

"That's gotta be a good feeling," he said.

"It is. I can't even describe how nice it is to go to work and enjoy what I'm doing and the people I work with. It might be the most relaxing environment that a person could work in."

"Ha, I bet! It's so quiet. And the couches and stuff. It would be like getting paid to hang out in the living room," Jackson said.

"Pretty much. And I love workin' with Donna, even though she can be a bit of a distraction sometimes," Reagan said.

"I'm so happy for you, hon. I can tell you've had less stress the last couple weeks."

"I know. Is it that obvious?" she asked.

"Yeah, but that's okay. You deserve it."

"I still feel bad about leaving Jen, though. But she swears she's gonna be workin' with her aunt soon. She's just waitin' for Angie to hire someone."

"That's nice of her," he said.

"I thought so, too. Hopefully, she hasn't killed any of the others yet," Reagan joked. "I'll call her later and see how it's been goin'."

She stared out the window, as the Camaro rolled south. Suddenly, she felt the warmth of Jackson's touch. He had laid his right hand on her left and weaved his fingers between hers. Reagan felt extraordinary bliss. The simple act of him taking her hand brought her comfort. She looked over at him. He glanced at her for as long as he could, before taking his gaze back to the road.

"What?" he said.

"Nothin'," she replied. "I was just wondering if you wanna hang out for a while when we get home?"

"I'll stay as long as you want me to," he replied.

"Forever?" she suggested. They exchanged a smile and Jackson squeezed her hand. The rolling tires hummed in their ears the rest of the way home.

CHAPTER 12

Before Reagan knew it, the vernal equinox had begun. Time at the library was flying and every day she went to work was like a child going to the playground. Jen had started her new job downtown, having thoroughly enjoyed the opportunity to give the girls one last piece of her mind. The warming climate had finally melted the snow and the birds seemed to have come back to life.

Jackson might as well have moved in with Reagan. They spent most of their free time together. His father frequently enjoyed her company and the opportunity to spoil her with his excellent cooking. He had eventually revealed some old photos of Jackson and, just as she had expected, he was adorable. She finally got to meet his brother, Dallas, who had come home one weekend. He was gone as fast as he had arrived.

Reagan woke up on this particular Monday in March, feeling a little lousy. She did her best to ignore her cramps and pushed through her normal morning routine. Her misery must have been noticeable to the world, though, because it didn't take Donna long to express her concern.

"Reagan, honey, are you all right?"

"Yeah, I'm fine. Just waiting on the medicine to kick in. I'm, you know . . ." She faded off as she grabbed her lower abdomen.

"Ah. Ick, sorry," Donna replied.

"Meh, it's been worse before. It'll get better."

"I hope so. That's no fun."

"Yup. Well, I'm gonna go put my stuff away and get to work," Reagan said.

"Okay, hon."

Reagan dropped her things off upstairs, then immediately went to check for returned books. The first couple of hours were agonizing but, as time passed and the medicine kicked in, she started to feel like her normal self. The optimistic aspect of the day was that she was going to meet Jackson at work for lunch. She had never been to the Holloway-owned business before, but it was only a five-minute drive from the library. When the time approached, Reagan went to the breakroom to get her lunchbox. She had made sandwiches for the two of them. With a quick wave to Donna, she strolled out the door and down the sidewalk to her car.

It wasn't long before she was approaching the construction company on the edge of town. There were several buildings on the property and about twenty vehicles lined up in the parking lot. Jackson's Camaro was alone in the corner. She was nervous about meeting him at work. Like usual, she was envisioning the worst, regarding what his coworkers would think of her. But if he had helped her with anything, it was to have more confidence in herself. So, she decided to hold her head up high and try her best to relax.

Reagan parked next to Jackson's car, then made her way across the asphalt to the nearest building. A sign that read "office" was posted above the door at the end. When she walked into the bedroom-sized space, a lady who appeared close to retirement age was sitting at a desk in the corner. There were two doors on the far wall. The first was labeled with a sign, indicating it was a restroom. The second had a plaque affixed with

David's name on it. She smiled, assuming he was sitting inside what must have been his office.

"Can I help you?" the woman asked.

"Hi. My name's Reagan Nichols. I'm here to eat lunch with Jackson."

"I can call for him . . ."

"That's okay. I told him I was on my way," Reagan said.

"All right, dear." The woman sat quietly, checking Reagan out over her glasses.

Suddenly, the second door opened, and David stepped out of his office. "Reagan!" he yelled in excitement. "When did you get here?" He wrapped her up in a hug.

"Just now," she answered. "I got a long lunch today, so I was gonna eat with Jackson," she told him, holding up the lunchbox.

"Cool. He'll like that. Does he know you're here?" David asked.

"Well, I told him . . ." she started.

"Oh, he's probably out back, cleanin' up. Come on, I'll take you."

"Okay," she replied, following his lead. She thanked the woman, before walking out with David. "This is really amazing," she told him.

"Thanks. I've spent half my life here. I can't imagine what it would be like without it," David told her.

"That's understandable. You've put so much of yourself into it."

"Ain't that the truth."

They entered the gravel lot behind the building. A handful of men were working inside a pole barn that sat off to the side. David and Reagan walked up to the open garage door. He leaned on the back of the truck that they were loading wood into.

"Hey, boys. Have you seen Jackson?"

The one standing closest to David looked over at him. "Yeah, I think he's back by the pallets."

"Thanks, Justin," David replied.

"Hey, boss," one of the other guys said. "I didn't know you had a daughter," he finished, with a smile.

"I don't. This is Reagan. She's Jackson's girlfriend," David told him.

"Ohhh, so you're the one he talks about constantly," the guy said to her. "You have any sisters?"

"Eli, knock it off," David instructed. He turned to Reagan and apologized, before making introductions. "Reagan, this is Justin, Eli, Toby, Logan, and Henry," he told her, as he gestured to each one by name.

"Nice to meet you all," she said politely.

All the guys gave her a casual wave or nod, except for one . . . Henry. He was about ten years older than the rest of them and looked like he hadn't slept in two weeks. She made eye contact with him for a moment, but looked away as fast as she could. Henry stared at her with the strangest expression she had ever seen. It was as though he had no emotion whatsoever. Everything about him made her uncomfortable, from the blank stare of his eyes to the awkward body language in his stance. She did everything she could to avoid meeting his gaze and followed David back outside.

Justin was right. Jackson was on the backside of the garage in a forklift, placing one last pallet on top of a human-sized stack. He caught Reagan and David in the corner of his eye and shut the forklift off.

"Sorry, I thought I could get done real quick. Did you wait long?"

"No. Your dad found me right after I got here, so he just brought me back. You can finish if you need to," she told him.

"Oh, I'm done. Let's eat. There are tables in the office. The guys shouldn't bother us too much," he said.

She laughed. "It's no problem. I met a few of them already."

A look of dread filled his face. "Oh, God. Eli didn't bother you, did he?"

Now she laughed even harder. "No, not really. But he's a character, for sure."

She found herself looking back in the garage door as they made their way across the gravel. None of the men were standing there anymore, which was a relief to her. Soon enough, she would find out why. When they walked into the breakroom, the deafening noise of the employees talking and potato chips crunching filled her ears. A small TV in the corner displayed the twelve o'clock news.

Jackson looked down at Reagan. "You sure you want to eat in here? They get pretty loud sometimes."

"Yeah, it's okay," she insisted.

"I'll be in my office, you guys. I got a couple more phone calls to make," David told them.

"All right, dad." Jackson and Reagan sat down at an empty table, then he jumped back up to get drinks from the refrigerator. "You want one?" he asked her.

"Yeah, thanks."

"This is all we got."

"It's perfect," she added.

"So, how's your day been?" he asked her.

"Okay, I guess. I mean, work's been fine. I felt a little crappy this morning, that's all," she told him.

"Oh, I'm sorry. Your stomach bothering you?"

"Nah, just . . . other stuff."

Jackson nodded. "Oh. That sucks. You feel any better?"

"Yeah, I'm good now. Took some meds," Reagan said.

"That's good," he said. "Sorry if I stink. I've been sweatin' all morning."

"You don't stink. And it's okay, you don't have to apologize," she told him.

"Thanks for bringing me lunch, by the way. Especially since you didn't feel good. You didn't have to do that."

"I don't mind. I was gonna feel like crap no matter what."

Both of them watched the news for a minute, while they ate

their sandwiches. Reagan took a drink of her pop and listened to the weather forecast. Although she focused her attention on the meteorologist, she kept feeling the urge to look across the room.

She knew that Henry was watching her again. She could feel his stare. Her gut told her to ignore it, but part of her had to verify that the feeling was right. She maintained her concentration on the screen, but no longer heard the sound of the news. She didn't hear the rowdy conversations from the other tables. The room started spinning. It seemed to darken. Finally, she gave in. Her green eyes moved from the TV on to him. And she was right . . . he was staring right at her. She looked away for a moment, then back at him again. His eyes moved from her face to every other inch of her body, then back to her face. Her heart began racing. She set her sandwich down on the napkin, her hands quivering.

Jackson looked over at her. "Reagan? Reagan?" He looked at her hands, then back at her face. A single tear had rolled down her right cheek. She looked down at her sandwich, unaware of how long she had been this way. "Reagan, are you okay?" She looked up at Jackson, her voice paralyzed. "You want me to take you home?" he offered.

She shook her head no.

"Do you need something?" he asked, desperately trying to help.

She shook her head again.

"You wanna eat somewhere else? You're scaring me, honey, what's wrong?"

She finally nodded yes.

"Okay, come on. We'll go out to my car for a minute," he told her.

"Okay." Reagan finally produced a sound.

The thought of even standing up was torture, but necessary. She put the sandwich back in the bag and forced herself to rise. Jackson being by her side was her only saving grace. He held her arm as they walked out of the room, through the front office, and across the parking lot. She had yet to speak when they reached his car. He took her trembling hand and stopped next to the passenger door.

"Christ, you're shaking. I'm taking you home," he insisted.

"No," she said. "Just give me a minute."

He wrapped her up in a hug, the most comforting one she had received in her entire life. Once she finally felt relaxed enough to express her disquiet, she lifted her head off his chest.

"Okay. One of the guys you work with, Henry, was really freaking me out."

"He's definitely a strange dude. What did he do?"

"Nothing, exactly. He just kept staring at me. I don't know how to explain it. It was like he wasn't human," Reagan said. "I swear to you, it's not me just being uncomfortable. I know I'm like that sometimes, but it wasn't that."

"No, I believe you. That guy's always been weird, and he's not even a hard worker. The only reason dad hired him is 'cause one of his buddies asked for a favor. And dad, as soft-hearted as he is, gave Henry a job. I'll talk to dad about it."

"No. Don't do that. It's not a big deal. He didn't really do anything except creep me out, and that's not a good enough reason to get him in trouble," she insisted.

"All right, fine. But I'll be watching him now. You can count on that."

She nodded in agreement, then laid her head against his chest again. The sound of his heartbeat was comforting. He caressed her back with his fingertips, nearly lulling her to sleep.

"Thanks, hon," she said.

"You feel better?" he asked.

"Yeah, thank you. I'm sorry. God, you're probably starving," she said.

He started laughing. "It's all right. We can eat still. Can you eat?"

"I don't know. I might eat a little later. My stomach's a little queasy right now. But I'll stay with you for lunch still, if you want."

"Yeah, as long as you're up for it. Come on," he said as he unlocked the car. They climbed in and he started it to let it warm up a little. "How long do you have?"

She looked at her watch. "About fifteen minutes. I need to be back by one."

"All right, well let's make it a great fifteen minutes." He turned on the radio and found the most upbeat music he could find. "Okay, how can I make Reagan feel better?" he asked out loud.

She immediately grinned at his irresistible charm. Even on what was panning out to be a pretty cruddy day, he could still manage to make her smile.

"Hmm, what did you have in mind?" she asked.

"Well, I didn't wanna have to tell you this, but I'm a terrible singer. However, if I have to sacrifice, I'll do it just this one time."

"Oh boy," she said.

"You'll be thinkin' "oh boy" in a minute," he said. "All right. Here we go. Here we go."

The song that was on the radio came to an end and another began. Reagan had no clue what the tune was, but it became apparent rather quickly that he did. Within a matter of seconds, he was singing the song to the best of his ability. She tried so hard to keep a straight face, but it was impossible. He hit exaggerated lows and screechy highs. It was quite possibly the most horrific yet beautiful thing she had ever heard. When all four and a half minutes of the song were finally complete, Reagan's uncontrollable laughter had her in tears yet again.

Jackson put down his imaginary microphone and let out the laughter that he had been holding in. "Wasn't that great?" he asked her.

She dabbed the tears from her eyes and took a deep breath, trying to regain control of her body. "That was amazing," she answered him, before busting up once more.

"I thought so, too," he agreed. "Don't worry, you can have my autograph."

"Oh, that would be amazing. Thanks, I feel so much better now."

"Good. That's what matters the most. The fact that I completely revealed this embarrassing side of myself means nothing," he joked. "Seriously, though, I love you. I just want you to feel better."

"I do now. And I love you, too."

After his heart-warming performance, Reagan's stomach had calmed a little, allowing her to take a few bites of her sandwich. They enjoyed their last few minutes together, before her time with him was up. She glanced at her watch again.

"Holy crap, that went fast," she told him.

"Time to go?" he asked.

"Yeah, I better get back."

"All right, baby," he replied. "I'm sorry it didn't go better."

"It's okay. It was worth it, just to get that once-in-a-lifetime treat," she told him.

"Once-in-a-lifetime is right," he said.

She grinned at him, hating the fact that she had to leave. "Well, I better go. I'll see you later, right?"

"I'll be there," he said.

They climbed out of his car and walked over to hers. She stopped at the door and turned to face him.

"Thanks again for the lovely song," Reagan said.

"That's what I'm here for, to make you smile," he said. He rested his right hand on the car and leaned in for a kiss. She melted on the spot; her entire body filled with butterflies. He pulled back and flashed her one more handsome grin. "I'll see you tonight," he added.

"Whew," she sighed, as if out of breath. "Okay." It was the only thing she could mutter after that.

Jackson gave her a final wave and headed back toward the office. Reagan started her car and made her way back to the library. She did the best she could to focus on the road, daydreaming about the touch of his lips. This amazing high carried her through the rest of the afternoon. The horrible experience had easily been trumped by the great one that Jackson left her with.

~

That evening, Jackson came over to hang out with Reagan, as promised. They ordered a pizza and started a movie. It didn't matter how often she rested against him on the couch, it never got old.

"Was the rest of your day better?" he asked.

"A lot better," she answered. "My body finally felt like I wasn't dying."

"That's good. I was gonna tell ya, that weirdo at work wouldn't even look at me the rest of the day."

"Really?"

He shook his head as he took another bite. "Nope. He's a coward. Wouldn't talk to me. Wouldn't look at me. I mean, he doesn't usually talk much anyway, but I could tell he was avoiding me like the plague."

"Weird," she said.

"You got that right," he replied.

"I'm sorry if I caused any trouble," she told him.

"You kiddin' me? You didn't do anything. He's the trouble," Jackson insisted.

"I know, I just don't get it. I don't understand why people act that way sometimes," Reagan said.

"Beats the hell out of me. I don't get it either."

Reagan finished her slice of pizza and got up to take her plate to the kitchen. "You want any more before I put it away?" she asked him.

"Nah. I might barf if I eat any more," he said.

She stuck the box in the fridge, then plopped back down on

the couch and leaned against him again. "I'm so glad you're here," she told him.

"Me too," Jackson replied.

He ran his fingers through her hair, twirling a strand around his index finger before letting it drop again. The repetitive action began to put her to sleep.

She looked up at him with fatigued eyes. "Will you stay here with me? Just for tonight."

He nodded, dropping the strand of hair down again. "Of course."

Reagan mumbled, "Okay," with whatever awareness she had left. Then her eyes closed.

CHAPTER 13

A couple of weeks passed by before Reagan stopped having thoughts about the nausea she had felt that day at lunch. They hadn't revisited what happened, nor had Jackson mentioned his coworker since that day. She planned to act as if it had never happened at all.

The trees hadn't quite filled with leaves yet, though the buds had given them a red hue. Daffodils and tulips painted Newbrook with color, something the town desperately needed after the cold, gray winter. Reagan adored the spring flowers. Her urge to create brush strokes on canvas escalated. The increased artistic activity had resulted in an ever-growing stock of paintings in her apartment.

"You're gonna run out of room," Jackson joked. "Look at you, creating all this beautiful art."

Reagan stood in the bathroom, in front of the mirror, wrapping a strand of hair around her curling iron. "You really think people will like them?" she asked.

"They will love them," he said from the living room. "Hey, I'm gonna take off. Dad will give me crap all day if I'm late."

"Okay. Love you," she said.

"Love you, too. See ya tonight," he said, before closing the door.

Reagan finished getting ready and walked out the door only a few minutes behind him.

She started her shift at work like any other day, but she had plans to leave around lunchtime.

"Oh, fun. The dentist," Donna remarked, when Reagan reminded her that she was taking off early.

"Yeah," Reagan replied, giving her friend a grimace. "But it's only a cleaning. No biggie."

"Piece of cake," Donna agreed.

Just as fast as Reagan had started work, she was leaving for the day. She checked in with Vickie before walking out and gave Donna a wave on her way out the door. She walked to her car, which was still sitting in front of her apartment building, and headed across town. About three blocks before the dentist's office, she spotted Jackson's crew working at a site downtown. She smiled, thinking it would be perfect to swing by and surprise him after her appointment.

Reagan was lucky enough to only spend a few minutes in the waiting room, and even more fortunate to get a thumbs up from the dentist. This wasn't unusual for her, as she had never had one cavity before, in the twenty-four years of her life. Getting antsier by the second, she checked out at the front desk, then rushed to her car, hoping to still find Jackson working up the road.

She rolled up a couple of minutes later and parked across the street, looking over to see if she could spot him amongst the crew. The hard hats made it slightly more difficult, but all it took was a small turn of his head to reveal his handsome face. She grinned, finding it pleasurable to watch him from afar for a few moments. He and Justin finished what they were working on, then stopped for a break. They walked over to the nearest truck to get in the cooler. This was the opportunity she was waiting for.

Reagan looked both ways before jogging across the street. Jackson tipped his head back, chugging the water he held in his left hand. Justin saw Reagan first and grinned at her, as she snuck up behind Jackson. She held her index finger up to her mouth, hoping he wouldn't give her away. He looked back at Jackson, pulling off a decent acting job. Reagan stepped up behind Jackson and ran her finger down his spine.

He nearly choked on his water and whipped around to face the culprit. She and Justin both laughed at his reaction.

"Reagan! You scared the shit out of me." He turned back to Justin. "Dude, you gotta tell me these things."

Justin laughed. "Sorry, man."

"Well, isn't this a pleasant surprise? What're you doing here?" he asked her.

"I had a dentist appointment right up the road. When I saw you working, I figured I would swing by for a sec," she told him.

"Oh, that's right. I forgot you were leaving early today. You gotta go back?" he asked.

"Nah, I took the rest of the day off. I'm gonna stop and see Jen before I go home."

"That's cool," he replied.

"Yeah. It's her birthday, so I got her a little something. And a cupcake."

"Well, that was nice of you. She'll like that," Jackson said.

"I hope so. Hey, look, I won't keep you long, I just wanted to say hi," Reagan told him.

"I'm glad you did. I'll see you tonight." He kissed her, then she waved goodbye to them as she jogged back to her car.

Her destination was a small antique store, across from the courthouse downtown. Jen's aunt had taken it over after her grandfather had passed several years back. Reagan was excited to see it, since she had never been there before. Not to mention she had a soft spot for antiques, especially if they involved art. The bell rang when Reagan walked in the door, a small box in one hand and a gift bag in the other.

"Welcome to Georg . . ." Jen started from the counter, until she looked up and saw her friend in front of the door. "Reagan! What brings you here?"

"I thought I'd bring my best friend something for her birthday," Reagan replied.

"Aww, you didn't have to do that," Jen said.

"I know, but it's the least I could do." Reagan handed Jen the items she had brought. "These are for you."

"Cool! Thanks, girl," Jen told her. She dug into the bag first. After a few sheets of tissue paper, she pulled out a t-shirt, labeled with the logo of her favorite band. "Oh, my God. Thanks, Reagan!" Jen exclaimed. "I've been lookin' for one of these."

The happiness of her friend filled Reagan with joy. "It's the least I could do after all you did for me," she said.

"Aww, thank you. And what's in here?" Jen asked. She opened the box, finding the oversized chocolate cupcake. "Damn, look at that! That looks awesome. Thank you so much." Jen walked out from behind the counter and wrapped Reagan up in a hug. Then she pulled back to check Reagan over. "You look good, girl. Not that you ever didn't. You're just glowing now," Jen said.

"Happiness. That's called happiness," Reagan replied.

Jen laughed. "Yeah, makes a big difference, doesn't it? So . . . how's it goin', you know, with you and your lover boy?" she said, nudging Reagan in the side.

Reagan blushed and grinned. "Good."

"Good?" Jen asked.

"Okay, great," Reagan restated. "He pretty much lives with me. Stays over all the time. Which I love, of course. I'm sure his dad misses him a little, but we eat dinner there all the time, so it balances out, I guess."

"Uh-huh, uh-huh," Jen replied. "I'm sure his dad's fine. I bet he cares more about how you guys are doing."

"He does. But I still feel sorry for him sometimes, ya know?"

"I get it, but I really think he'll be okay knowing you two are happy," Jen said. "How's the new job, by the way?"

"Great. I love it so much. I took off early today 'cause I had to go to the dentist."

"Oh bummer, but at least you got part of the day off, right?"

"Yeah, true. I'm gonna stop and get groceries on the way home. Take advantage of shopping during the daytime," Reagan told her.

"That's the best time to go. Or in the morning," Jen added.

"Exactly. Anyway, the job is perfect for me. It doesn't feel like I'm working. I still cringe when I think about the mall, though, I can tell ya that," Reagan said.

Jen shivered. "Bleh, me too."

"How's it goin' for you here?" Reagan asked.

"Awesome. I love it. It's so laid back. And it's pretty interesting sometimes. We get some pretty cool stuff."

"I bet. Where's your aunt?"

"In the back," Jen said. "She'll be out in a little bit. She's checkin' out some new things we got in."

"Oh. Okay. You care if I look around for a minute?" Reagan asked.

"Go for it," Jen said.

Reagan took a lap around the room, catching up with Jen along the way. She picked up and examined a few items here and there, unsure of what she wanted to buy. On the back wall, an old, hand-carved, empty picture frame was hanging on display. It immediately caught her eye.

"Wow! Look at this," she told Jen. "I really like this."

"I bet she'll give you a good deal on it," Jen said.

"I'll just pay for it. It's all right," Reagan insisted.

"Are you sure?" Jen asked.

"Yeah, it's okay." Reagan finished looking around, picking up a couple small things on her way back to the counter. "Okay, I'll take all of this," she said.

"If you say so, ma'am," Jen joked.

"I insist," Reagan added. "How much do I owe ya?"

Jen crunched the numbers on the old cash register. "Thirty-two, hon."

"That's not bad at all," Reagan said as she swiped her card.

"Here ya go," Jen said, handing her the bag and receipt. "Thank you so much for the shirt and the cake. I'm glad you stopped by. I didn't realize how much I missed seein' ya."

"Ditto. You know you can come over any time you want. If you wanna hang out or watch a movie, just call me," Reagan told her.

"I might take you up on that," Jen replied. "I wouldn't want to intrude on you guys, though."

"Heck, Jackson wouldn't care. He always thought you were cool."

"Aww, that's nice of him. Well, I'll call you some time then," Jen told her.

"Sounds good. I'll see ya later," Reagan said.

"Bye," Jen replied.

Reagan climbed back in her car and gently laid the bag on the passenger seat. Her last stop was conveniently on her way back to the apartment. Just as she had suspected, the parking lot at the store was practically vacant, and the inside matched. She stood in the meat department for about five minutes longer than she intended to, attempting to choose what to make for supper. After finally picking out some pork chops, she finished weaving through the aisles to get the rest.

Just after three o'clock, Reagan walked into her apartment, then made two trips to the car to carry the groceries in. If anything was worse for her than buying the groceries, it was the process of putting them away. When she finally finished, she went ahead and hopped in the shower to get it out of the way. She donned her favorite flannel pants and an old t-shirt, turned on the TV for noise, and stuck a new piece of canvas on the easel.

It became clear to her in no time why she didn't like daytime television. Fortunately, it was quite rare that she had to worry about it. Reagan prepared a variety of colors on the palette and laid out a few brushes of different sizes. She started with a light tint of blue and a large brush. With the gentle touch of her hand, she dipped the brush into the paint, then stretched her arm up until the bristles grazed the canvas.

A knocking sound echoed off the walls of the apartment. Reagan turned her head and looked at the TV. A fast-food commercial advertised French fries and fountain pop. She raised her hand back up, then another couple of knocks interrupted her concentration. Reagan looked at her watch and laid the brush down, then stood up and headed toward the door.

"Jackson, you didn't have to leave work early, just 'cause I'm home." She unlocked the deadbolt and turned the knob. "I won't complain . . ." she trailed off.

Her front door opened with force, pushing her backward. She looked up, getting a glance at the person in the black mask rushing toward her. Reagan gasped as the taser was plunged into her body.

CHAPTER 14

Nearly two and a half hours later, Jackson knocked on the door of Reagan's apartment. He waited for a second for her to get the door. When she didn't answer, he reached down and turned the unlocked knob. He walked in and closed it behind him.

"I made it, finally. Sorry, I went home first, and dad insisted on arguing with me about the damn weather tomorrow. I swear he looks for a reason to argue with me." Jackson looked down the hallway toward the bathroom. "Reagan?" He scrunched his face in confusion. "Reagan?" he called, louder the second time.

Only silence filled her apartment, disrupted by the occasional car engine passing by outside.

Jackson walked down the hall and looked in the bathroom – empty. He looked in her bedroom across the hall – empty. He hurried back out to the living room and pulled the curtain back on the window that faced the small parking lot. Her car was sitting in its usual spot. Jackson's heart started pounding and he struggled to breathe. He started back across the room, then something caught his eye, stopping him in his tracks. The canvas she had placed on the easel remained as she had left it. Jackson gazed at the single brushstroke of blue across the top of the canvas. The palette and brush, still colored with paint that was starting to dry, were lying on a small table next to her chair. He lifted the brush, noticing the clumpy paint clinging to the bristles. It started to shake in his trembling hand, and he struggled to hold on to it. He laid the brush down and reached for the phone in his pocket.

He called Reagan's phone, hoping to get some kind of answer. The phone rang from the bedroom. Jackson ran down the hall and turned the corner short, slamming his shoulder into the doorframe. His heart sank when he spotted the pink phone on top of the dresser. He stepped forward and grasped it in his hand. With quivering fingers, he found Jen's number and called it. The phone only rang once before she answered it.

"Hey, girl," Jen answered.

"Uh . . ." Jackson started.

"Hello?" Jen asked.

"Jen?" he verified.

"Yeah. Who's this?"

"This is Jackson. I'm Reagan's boyfriend."

"Oh, hi," she said with a chuckle. "I knew her voice wasn't that deep," she joked. Jackson struggled to speak, as hard as he wanted to. "Is something wrong?" Jen asked. The tone of her voice changed completely.

"I . . . I don't know. I was hoping she was with you, but . . ."

"Reagan? No, I saw her this afternoon at the store. Then she said she was goin' to get groceries. Why?" Jen asked.

"She's not, she's not here," Jackson stuttered, trying hard to choke back tears.

"She's not home?"

"No. Her car's here. And her phone was on the dresser. But she's not here. I don't know where she is." Jackson was in tears at this point. He started pulling at his hair with his left hand. Beads of sweat formed on his forehead.

"Okay. Try to stay calm. Maybe she had to run out for something and forgot her phone," Jen suggested. "The library!" she called out. "Did you check the library?" she asked.

"No. You're right, she always walks there." He looked at his watch. "I think they're still open. I'm gonna go. Thank you," he told her.

"Call me back and let me know," Jen said.

"I will," he said, running out the door. "Bye."

He sprinted down the steps, skipping two at a time. He moved as fast as his legs would take him, down the sidewalk and up the library steps. With only ten minutes to spare before closing time, he rushed through the doors. The lady behind the counter let out a shriek at the sound of the wood hitting the doorstop. He stumbled up to the counter, out of breath, his face dripping wet. The silver-haired woman trembled with fear.

"Reagan . . ." he paused, trying to breathe. "Is Reagan here?"

"Reagan works during the day, dear. She left hours ago. I'm retired. I only work here part-time in the evenings," she said.

"Yes, but is she here?" he pressed. "Did she come back for something? Have you seen her?"

"No. I have not. Can you please lower your voice, sir?"

"Sorry. Please, you haven't seen her at all?" he tried again.

"I'm sorry. Is something wrong?" she asked in concern. He raised both hands to his face and receded until his back hit the door. "Sir?" she called as she watched him walk out.

Jackson stumbled back down the steps. He paced back and forth on the sidewalk, thinking, racking his brain for any clue as to where she could be. He pulled his phone back out and redialed Jen.

"Hello?" she answered immediately.

"She's not here!" he screamed. "She's not at the library. Something's wrong. She left paint out. She never does that. I don't know where she is," he cried out. His thoughts were racing faster than he could keep up.

"All right, Jackson, I think you need to call the police," Jen told him.

He sobbed. The reality of the situation hit hard with the word "police".

"Oh my, God," he cried.

"Jackson, call the police. It still may be nothing. She may have just walked to the dollar store or something. But if you call them, they can help you look for her. Okay?"

"Okay. Okay, I'll call them," he told her.

"Alright. Let me know if you hear anything. I'll go out and drive around for a while and look. Okay?"

"Okay. Thank you," he said.

Jackson hung up the phone, then dialed 9-1-1. He stared at the number for a second in disbelief at what he was about to do. Then he pushed the green button.

"9-1-1, what's your emergency?" the operator asked. He took a deep breath, trying to think of what to say. "Hello?" the operator asked.

"Yes, I don't know . . ." he began. "My girlfriend's missing. I don't know where she is," he cried.

"Alright, sir. It's okay. What's her name?"

"Reagan Nichols," he answered.

"Okay," she said, typing in the background. "And you are?"

"Jackson Holloway." He walked slowly back toward the apartment building.

"You're at her address on Market?"

"Yes."

"Are you certain she's missing, sir? Could she be at a friend's house? With family perhaps?" the operator asked.

"No, no, I don't think so. Her car and phone are here. Her parents live two hours away. And I already called the only person that she would go see. She wasn't there either."

"Okay. Is there anything suspicious in her house? Signs of a struggle? Anything unusual?" she continued.

"I didn't see anything like that. But it looked like she started a painting, then stopped suddenly. That seemed weird to me. Even if she had to leave, she wouldn't leave her brush and stuff like that. And her car is here. Why would she leave her car here?"

"I don't know, sir. I'm just trying to help talk this through. Is there anyone that could have picked her up? Any other friends or coworkers?"

"There's one coworker that she's kind of close to, but I don't think they've ever talked outside of work before. Something is wrong, I'm telling you," he insisted. His frustration and fear radiated through his voice.

"Okay, I believe you, sir. Please try to stay calm. There's an officer on the way over now. I promise they will do their best to handle the situation," the operator reassured him.

"Okay, thank you," he replied nervously.

"I will stay on the line with you until they arrive, then we can disconnect."

He looked down the street at the headlights moving in his direction. The sun was creating just enough light to see, but not enough to see well. He squinted.

"I think they're here now." The police car pulled up in front of the building. "Yeah, they're here."

"Okay, sir. They will assist you now. Good luck to you," the operator said.

"Thanks." Jackson hung up the phone and faced the officer walking toward him.

"Good evening," the officer said. "You must be Jackson."

"Yes, ma'am," he answered.

"I'm Officer Baker. You believe you have a missing person to report?" she asked.

"Yes, my girlfriend, Reagan Nichols. Maybe. I guess I don't know for sure. I just know something's not right," he told her.

"Alright. Walk me through what happened," the officer requested.

"Um. We got up and went to work this morning. She left work early and went to the dentist," he explained.

"You live here with her?" she asked.

"No, not technically. I'm here a lot, though."

"Do you know when and where her appointment was?"

"I'm pretty sure it was at twelve-thirty. She goes to Morris Dentistry," he said. "Then she stopped in to see me at the construction site about three blocks away."

"What time was that?"

"It was after one. One-fifteen maybe."

"Okay," she said, making notes as he talked.

"Then she went to the George's Antique Store downtown to visit her friend, Jen. She works there. I called her a little bit ago and she said Reagan had been there this afternoon, then she was gonna get groceries and go home," he told her.

"Alright. What time did you get here?" Officer Baker asked.

"Not that long ago. It was a little after six."

"Okay, Jackson. Let's go in and take a look around."

Jackson led her inside, waiting on her next question. She walked through the apartment, examining the different rooms, taking notes. She stopped at the easel and gazed at the brush and palette lying next to it.

"That's why I think something is wrong," Jackson said. "I mean, we've only been together for four months, but I've never seen her start a painting, then just leave the paint and brush like that. It's not like her at all."

"You're right, it is a little strange. There are no signs of a struggle, though. No signs of a break-in. Other than this, did you notice anything out of place? Anything missing?" she asked.

"No, not really," he answered. "No one has seen her, though. I went to the library; she works there. They hadn't seen her since she left at lunch today. Jen hadn't seen her since she left the store. Why would she come home and leave without her car and her phone?" he asked in frustration.

"I'm not saying that's what happened. I'm only trying to find as many pieces of the puzzle as possible," she told him. He took a deep breath and nodded. "Have you talked to her parents?" she continued.

"No. I didn't want to alarm them yet. They're two hours away, so . . ."

"I understand, but we do need to contact them to confirm that they haven't seen her."

"Okay," he said.

"All right, here's what we're gonna do. I need any information you can give me about her family, friends, and work. Any contact information you can give me will be helpful. Any enemies she may have. Anything unusual at all. I will be in contact with all of these people tonight. I'll also get in touch with the landlord in the morning to see if there are any security cameras or footage that we can review. In the meantime, as hard as it may be, we need you to be patient. There's only so much we can do at this point. The reality is, she was last seen only five hours ago. I know it seems unlikely, but she may still show up. It is possible that she left of her own free will," the officer told him.

Jackson nodded, although in complete disagreement with her last statement. He walked over to the kitchen, opened the junk drawer, and pulled out a piece of scrap paper and a pencil. Reagan's phone in hand, he started jotting down the contacts that the officer had requested.

"May I see that for a second when you're done?" she asked.

"Sure." He handed it to her after he finished his list.

"Well, it doesn't look like she had any recent calls or messages," she said, examining the phone before handing it back to him. "If you hear anything or have any information at all, you call me." She handed Jackson her card.

"Okay," he replied. "Thank you."

"Either way, I will be in touch with you tomorrow. If nothing changes between now and then, we will open a case. All right?"

He nodded in agreement, looking down at his feet.

She turned and walked out of the apartment, closing the door behind her.

Jackson stood in the kitchen after she had pulled away, still looking down at his shoes. He slammed his fist on the counter in frustration at the hopelessness that devastated him. His mind was racing as fast as his heart. He finally left the room, not knowing what he should do or where to go. Eventually, he stepped into Reagan's room and sat down on the bed. A pink sweater lay next to him. He rested his hand on the sweater, before lifting it to his face. With a deep inhale through his nose, he took in her scent, and it was more than he could digest. Jackson gripped the sweater until his knuckles turned white, his tears falling into the fabric. Several minutes passed before he was able to breathe normally again.

He reached for Reagan's phone once again, calling Jen for the third time.

"Jackson?" she asked.

"Yeah, it's me. Any luck?" he asked.

"No. I'm sorry, I haven't seen her," Jen told him. "What did the police say?"

"They asked a lot of questions, walked around, got some information. Basically, she said if we haven't heard from her by morning, then they'll open a case."

"Okay. Look, I'm gonna stay out for a little bit longer. Let me know if anything changes," she said.

"I will. Thank you for helping, Jen. You're such a good friend," Jackson told her.

"It's not a problem. I just wish I could do more."

"Me too. That's what's killing me the most. I can't help her."

"You are. You're doing everything you can possibly do right now," she reassured him.

"Yeah . . . All right, I'm gonna go. I'll let you know if I hear something," Jackson told her.

"Okay. Try to get some rest."

"I'll try." Jackson hung up. As much as he hated to do it, he now took out his phone and made another call.

"Hello?" his dad answered.

"Dad . . ." Jackson started, unable to make any other words.

"Jackson, what's wrong?" David asked immediately. The only sound Jackson could produce for a moment was the sniffling from his nose. "Jackson?" his dad asked again.

"She's gone, dad. Something happened to her."

"What? Who? Reagan? What do you mean, she's gone?"

"She's gone. I can't find her. No one knows where she is," Jackson told him.

"I'm sure it's all right. Maybe she had to run out for something," David suggested.

"Her car's here. Something happened to her."

"Call the police, Jackson."

"I did. They just left."

"All right. What did they say?" his dad asked.

"They took a bunch of information and said if she doesn't show up tonight, they'll look into it tomorrow," Jackson answered. "I hate it. I feel like I can't do anything but sit here and wait. What if she's hurt? What if . . .?"

"Jackson, listen to me. You're not gonna help the situation any with "what ifs". You've done everything you can do right now. I know that's not what you want to hear, and I'm sorry."

"I know. What am I supposed to do? Should I go out and look for her? Should I call her parents?" Jackson begged for his father's advice.

"Honestly, you should probably stay put, just in case. Even if you go out, you wouldn't even know where to look. You may want to call her parents, though. Talk to them. Let them know that they've got your support. They will need that comfort, trust me," David advised him.

"Okay. I will."

"You need to tell me if you need anything. If you want me to stay there with you, I will," his dad offered.

"Thanks, dad. I'll be okay."

"Alright, bud. I'll be prayin' for her. And I love you."

"Love you, too," Jackson replied.

Jackson gave himself a minute to prepare, before calling Reagan's parents. When they answered, he could tell the officer had already contacted them. He tried his best to stay strong, reassuring them that he would do whatever he had to do to find Reagan. Once Barbara calmed her emotions, she let him know that they would be down in the morning, then they hung up for the night.

By the time he got off the phone for the evening, it was a quarter to nine. Jackson paced the floor, not knowing what else to do at that point. He wasn't hungry, he didn't want to leave, and he didn't feel like hearing the TV. He sat on the couch in the dark room, staring out the window. His mind had gone numb enough that he stopped producing tears. It was as if his body and soul were paralyzed. He fought the fatigue for hours, still sitting on the middle couch cushion. His body eventually wore down and he slumped over on the decorative pillow, closing his tired eyes.

Jackson sat up, startled, gasping for air. He looked at the clock, now showing 4:22. A few seconds later, the roaring engine of the diesel truck on the street echoed off the buildings, revealing the cause for his disrupted sleep. He made his way to the restroom, then finally decided to turn on the TV. A cruddy sitcom rerun was playing, a sure sign that it was four in the morning. As much as his disinterest tempted him to change the channel, his hand didn't budge on the remote. He found himself staring again, the words of the actors ringing in his ears.

"God, will you look at that guy?" the brunette woman on the show said to the girl jogging next to her. *"What's his deal?"*

"He's a creepo," the other woman replied.

Jackson gasped, standing straight up as fast as his legs would let him. The girls' conversation continued in the background. He watched the screen for another moment before sprinting into the kitchen. Jackson pinched the business card between his thumb and index finger, reading the phone number on the front. He called the number. Every time the phone rang, he grew more anxious. *Answer. Answer. Please answer.*

"Hello?" a sleepy voice spoke.

"I know who it was!" he said. "I know who took her."

"You know who took her?" Officer Baker asked, more alert this time.

"Yes. It was Henry Booker, I'm sure of it. He works with me."

CHAPTER 15

The four tiny feet of one plump rat scurried along Reagan's flannel pants. She was lying on a concrete floor. Her eyelids twitched, the tickling sensation starting to wake her. She slowly opened her eye, just enough to let in some hazy light. Her irises rolled back and forth for a moment. Then she clenched her eyelids tight, lifted her head off the floor, and opened her eyes fully.

As she regained consciousness, the reality of her environment began to set in. The tape over her mouth restricted her breathing, which had accelerated. Reagan's eyes started to focus inside the dim room. She looked down at the rat, which had paused in its journey, and her throat attempted a shriek at the sight of it. Her ankles had been taped, but she did the best she could to kick her legs. Both of her arms were bound together behind her back. It was a struggle, but she gradually maneuvered her body into a sitting position.

After several deep breaths through her nose, Reagan looked around the room. Cold tears rolled down her quivering cheeks. She couldn't make out many details. Only one beam of light shined in from a security light outside. The rays entered through a miniature window near the ceiling. There didn't seem to be much in the room besides some shelves on the nearest wall and a broken chair, discarded in the corner. An awful, musty smell lingered in the air. Other than the scratching of rodents and the distant dripping of water, the room was scarily quiet.

Reagan sat alone in the dark, thinking, problem-solving. The only thing she could contemplate doing was to make her way to the shelves to try to find something, anything, that could help her situation. She used her heels and buttocks to scoot across the dusty floor until she approached the old wooden ledges. There wasn't much on the bottom one, other than an old pair of shoes and a cardboard box. Both looked like they had been there for a decade. The next shelf up was a little more promising. Four Mason jars sat in a row. They too looked as if they had been there a long time. She raised her brows, hopeful that a broken jar could help her out. If only she could knock one down.

The silence was suddenly interrupted. Footsteps creaked on the wooden boards above Reagan's head. Clouds of dust drifted down with every step. She stopped moving, her heart rate doubled, and her chest trembled with every exhale. She listened as quietly as possible. The sound of the steps made their way across the room to the other side. It grew quiet again, only for a moment, then she heard keys. A padlock jostled on a door she couldn't see. Another tear rolled down her face as she waited for the door to open.

A sudden burst of light shone down on the floor like a spotlight. Reagan turned her back toward the shelves. The horrible reality of her situation began to sink in, knowing all she could do was sit there. Each wooden stair creaked under the weight of the stranger, who was slowly making their way down to her. She trembled, completely overrun with fear.

Finally, the dark figure turned the corner and stood before her. His face was obscured at first from the shadow cast by the light at his back. Reagan squinted up at him, unable to focus on his features.

"Don't be frightened, Reagan," he said. "As long as you behave yourself, you have nothing to worry about."

He took a couple more steps, now standing right at her feet. She forced her back against the shelves and pulled her knees up to her chest, doing her best to keep space between them.

Henry crouched down, his face entering the light from the stairway. Reagan tried to scream, but the tape locked her lips together.

"Shhh," he said, wiping a tear away from her cheek. "I know you don't think this now, but I *will* take care of you. You'll see in time that I can be the man any woman dreams of."

Reagan shook her head, disgusted by everything about him and the words spewing from his mouth.

"But until you realize and accept that, you're giving me no choice but to keep you like this."

He stopped talking. She looked upon his face with fearful eyes and he stared back at her, grinning at the corner of his mouth.

"God, you're beautiful," he continued. "I bet he doesn't even know it. But I see it. I appreciate your beauty, Reagan."

Henry reached up and grabbed a strand of her hair, allowing it to flow through his hand. She grimaced, his touch sickening her to the core.

"Now I'm gonna go get you some water and take this tape off. And before you get any wise ideas, there isn't anyone around for about a mile. Don't waste your breath."

He stood and made his way back up the creaky steps. The combination of his unnerving presence and the cold, damp air caused even the tiniest muscles in her body to twitch. All she could think of was the warmth of Jackson's arms holding her. Only a few moments later, Henry started back down the steps. He crouched back down in the same spot he had occupied before.

"I'm sorry if this hurts," he said.

He raised his right hand to her cheek and pinched the corner of the tape. She cringed as he slowly pulled the strip back until it released.

As much as she thought she would scream or fill his ears with the thousands of words that flooded her mind, she didn't make a sound. He lifted a glass of water and aimed the straw at her mouth.

"Here, take a drink," he advised her.

She looked at the glass, then back at him.

"No," she told him.

"You need to drink something," he instructed, in nurse-like fashion.

With spite, she replied, "I don't have to do anything."

He appeared surprised at first, then smiled again. "You see, this is one of the things I like about you. You're quiet and gentle, but strong when you need to be."

"You don't know anything about me."

"I know more than you think," he told her. "One more chance, then I'm takin' it back upstairs." She stared back at him, speechless. "Okay, suit yourself." He grinned, then picked the Mason jars off the shelf. "I'll take these, too."

"Alright, I'll take a drink," she said.

"Atta girl."

Henry set the jars back down, then squatted again. He held the glass up and aimed the straw at her mouth. She leaned in, Henry watching her every move as she pressed her lips against the plastic tube. She filled her mouth with water, released the straw, then sprayed the liquid all over his face. His stimulated expression instantly turned to one of rage.

"Bitch!"

He struck the left side of her face and her limp body fell to the cold floor in a cloud of dust.

CHAPTER 16

J ackson paced in the living room, waiting, sweating. Finally, a knock on the door interrupted his pattern. He sprinted to the foyer and swung the door open in a hurry, facing the officer he had spoken to earlier.

"It was him. It was him," he started, as if he had never hung up the phone.

"All right, slow down," she told him. "Start by telling me who this man is and why you believe he is responsible."

"Henry Booker is his name, or at least that's what he says. We work together at my dad's construction company."

"Okay," she said, taking notes again. "What's the name of your dad's company?"

"Holloway Construction," he replied.

"All right, Jackson. What led you to think he abducted Reagan?"

"Back in March, she came to work one day to each lunch with me. We were sitting in the breakroom and, all of a sudden, she looked like she'd seen a ghost. Her whole body was shaking. She could hardly speak. It scared the crap out of me. Anyway, I asked her what was wrong. She wouldn't even answer me. I took her out to my car and that's when she

138

finally said that Henry had been staring at her from across the room."

"Okay. With all due respect, that doesn't sound all that unusual. Was he making gestures at her?" the officer asked.

"No, I don't think so. I don't know. I didn't see it. But I'm telling you, I saw the fear in her eyes. I felt her hands shaking. She was scared to death. Whatever he was doing really messed her up. I had to horribly embarrass myself to make her feel better." The officer looked at him quizzically. "I had to sing," he clarified.

"Okay," she said, smiling at him. "So, what did she end up telling you?"

"She said that he was staring at her and wouldn't look away. Like he wasn't human."

"Did anything happen after that? Any other occurrences?" she asked.

"No, but she never came around after that. And he avoided me like the plague from that day on." He paused for a second to gather his thoughts. "Until yesterday . . ."

"What?"

"Yesterday was the first time she had been around the crew since the day he did that. When she stopped to see me at the worksite. But he was workin' on the other side. I don't know if he even knew she was there." His stomach tangled in knots at the thought that crossed his mind next. "He followed her. I bet he followed her when she left and no one noticed, 'cause he's worthless, anyway. That son-of-a-bitch!"

"All right, Jackson. Listen, I'm gonna go speak with the landlord, check if they have any footage that I can review from yesterday. And I will pay a visit to Henry, to see if there's anything suspicious about him. Hang in there, okay? We're gonna do everything we can. Please stay in touch with me if you need to, and I will most certainly be contacting you when I get some information." she finished.

"Yes. Thank you," he replied.

She left and he went right back to pacing the apartment. About thirty minutes later, another knock on the door shocked him. There was no way she was back already.

"Jackson, it's me," David called from outside the door.

Jackson let his father in and locked the door behind him. "I thought you'd be on your way to work," he said to him.

"I was. I thought I should check on you. I'm worried about you, son."

"Don't worry about me. Worry about her. That asshole took her."

David furrowed his brows. "Who?"

"Henry. I know he did it, dad. That crazy bastard followed her and took her. I swear I'm gonna kill him," Jackson said. "Was he at work?"

"He called in sick today," David said.

"Of course he did!" Jackson screamed.

"I'm confused. What makes you think Henry did it?"

"I just know. I know by the way he made her feel. I should have done something about it then, but I didn't. I let it go."

"There wasn't anything you could have done, Jackson. Other than a creepy look, there wasn't anything to question him about," David told him.

"I could have told him to keep his filthy eyes off her."

"Then what?" David asked. "Would it have changed anything?"

Jackson leaned against the back of the couch, stewing. "No."

"Did you call . . ." David began.

"Yes. They were here already. I told her everything. She said she's goin' to talk to him now. We'll find out how sick that bastard really is." Jackson stared off into space. David remained quiet, watching his son from the other side of the room. "Oh, God. Dad . . ." he said, before breaking down in tears.

David rushed over to his son and held him up from the force of pain and gravity trying to bring him down.

"Shhh," his father told him, caressing Jackson's back. "It's gonna be all right. She's gonna be okay. They'll find her. They *will* find her. You hear me?"

Jackson nodded, his head resting on his father's shoulder. He lay still, taking in the scent of his father's cologne.

"When is the pain gonna stop?" Jackson asked. He pulled his head back and stared into his father's eyes. "How much pain do we have to go through, dad? I don't think I can lose someone again."

David's despair and empathy for his son's heartache projected through the expression on his face. He pulled him in again, squeezing him tight. They stood together in the living room, waiting for some kind of relief. David eventually left, having desperately tried to get Jackson to come home with him for a while, to get some rest. Jackson stayed, though, unable to walk away from Reagan's space.

A tortuous two more hours passed before he heard the glorious sound of knocks again. He let Officer Baker in, praying inside for any good news she could give him. Jackson gazed at her with helpless, darkened eyes.

"Let's sit down, Jackson," she said.

They took a seat at the table. Jackson's knee bounced up and down as he waited on her to tell him something good.

"Well, I can verify for you now that someone was here yesterday," she said. His heart rate escalated at the sound of her words. "I watched the footage from the camera at the end of the hall, as well as the one at the entrance to the building."

"Okay," he said, both dreading and awaiting her next words.

"There was a suspect, most likely male, that entered the building yesterday at three forty-six pm. They can be seen again approaching her door and leaving . . ." She paused then restarted, ". . . leaving with her in their arms."

Jackson began crying again. He had lost track of how many times he had cried in the last day.

"Wait, why do you keep saying "they"? You don't know who it is?"

"The suspect was wearing a mask with black paint underneath. At no point in any of the footage can you see their face or even their skin color. All we can do is estimate physical features, such as height and weight. From this alone, it is most likely a male," she informed him. "No vehicle was identified. We're unsure which direction the suspect approached from."

His frustration intensified. "But what about Henry?" he demanded. "You said you were gonna go talk to him."

"I did. He was home, apparently with some type of cold. Believe me, Jackson, I questioned him. There was nothing suspicious about him or any of his answers," she said. Jackson looked at her in disgust, wondering how the twisted man could have pulled it off. "I asked him if I could come in and take a look around," she continued.

"Okay?"

"I checked every room, every closet . . . there was no sign of her. There wasn't anything suspicious enough to arrest him."

"You've gotta be shittin' me!" he exclaimed.

"I even talked to your dad, Jackson. He told me Henry called in sick today," she said.

"It's an act! He planned it all. He knew you would be there. You can't fall for that," he demanded. "Just 'cause she wasn't there, doesn't mean he didn't do it."

"You're right. And he isn't out of the question. We just need more evidence first. Please try to be patient . . ."

"Patient?" he repeated.

"I know that's asking for a lot. I can't imagine the pain and frustration you feel. Hear me now, we aren't going to let this go. We have to investigate the crime completely and take all possibilities into account. Unfortunately, this is a process that usually takes time," the officer said.

"How in the hell did he walk out of here, carrying a human being?" he asked. "Did no one notice?"

"Honestly, I'm not sure. I found it hard to believe, as well."

Jackson rested his elbows on his knees and his face in his

hands. The fatigue, fear, and devastation continued to wear him down.

"What am I supposed to do now?" he asked.

"I don't know what to say that will help. From the look of it, you could use some rest. And maybe a meal. Don't forget to take care of yourself," she advised him. He sat still, unaffected by her words of wisdom. "All right, Jackson. I will contact you if we get any new information."

She patted him on the back, then left the apartment. Jackson remained slumped over for ten minutes after she departed. He replayed the information she had given him over and over, trying to think of how the monster got away with it.

More than twelve hours had passed since he had made the dreaded phone call to 9-1-1. Now, after much deliberation, Jackson decided to take a drive. He didn't know where to go or what to do. He didn't want to go home. He didn't want to venture out far. Jackson merely needed a chance to breathe for a little while. Up and down the streets of Newbrook, his tires rolled without a destination. He felt like he was lost in the town he had grown up in. More than twenty stop-signs later, his phone began to ring. Barbara Nichols' name was displayed on the screen. He closed his eyes for a moment, dreading having to pick up the call.

"Hello?" he answered.

"Jackson?" a very upset voice replied on the other end.

"Hey, I'm sorry I haven't called yet this morning, Mrs. Nichols. My head's been spinning."

"It's okay, dear. I just wanted to check in with you. We spoke with the officer . . . the one you've been talking to. She told us . . ." She paused, crying in the background. "She told us that Reagan was taken."

"Yeah. I'm so sorry. I don't even know what to say," he told her.

"I know, honey. It's okay. There isn't much to say right now. All we can do is stay strong and have faith," she encouraged.

"I'm trying," he replied.

"It's going to be all right. We were going to come down, but we may wait until we speak to the police again. She said there isn't a lot we can do," Barbara said.

"She's right," he told her. "It doesn't matter if you're here or there, you feel like you can't do anything to help."

"She did say she was a little concerned about you, though."

"I'll be fine. I'm just worried about Reagan," he replied.

"I understand that, but she wouldn't want you to feel bad," Barbara said.

"I know she wouldn't," he said. "I had to leave for a minute and clear my head. I'll try to rest when I get back."

"Well, I'll let you go for now, then. That way you're not talking while you're trying to drive. We'll talk later, okay?"

"Okay."

"Hang in there," she added.

"You, too," he said.

"Bye, dear."

"Bye."

Jackson stayed out until almost ten. He made his way around town three times before finally stopping back at the apartment. Another phone began ringing from his pocket; this time it was Reagan's. He gasped, fumbling through his jacket pocket, trying to answer it before the ringing stopped.

"Hello?" he said.

"Hello? Um, I was trying to reach Reagan," a woman's voice said.

He pulled the phone back to look at the name. *Newbrook Library* lit up on the screen.

"Is this Donna?" he asked her.

"Yes . . ." she said hesitantly.

"This is Jackson," he finally told her.

"Oh, hi." She started laughing. "Sorry, I was confused for a second."

"Ha, yeah, I can understand that," he replied, trying to sound normal.

"Anyway, I was wondering where Reagan is. It's not like her to not show up for work. Is she feelin' okay?" Donna asked.

"Uh, I . . . Sorry, I thought they called you already," he said.

"What? Who?"

"Donna . . . Reagan was abducted yesterday. The police are looking for her," Jackson told her.

"Oh, my God! Oh, Reagan . . ." Donna burst into tears.

Jackson gave her a moment to process the news. "Donna, I'm so sorry. I should have called you sooner."

She sniffled. "It's okay. Oh, I hope she's all right."

"Me, too. She's strong. We just have to be strong for her, too," Jackson said.

"Okay. I will."

"I will call you if I hear anything. I promise," he told her.

"Thank you. Let us know if you need anything. Anything at all. We're here for you."

"Thanks, Donna. Bye."

Jackson hung up the phone and climbed out of the car. His legs felt heavy, the exhaustion starting to catch up. Each stair exaggerated the weakness that he felt. When he finally made it inside the apartment, he stumbled into the living room and collapsed onto the couch.

Reagan's body lay limp on a sheet of plywood. She opened her eyes, but the complete darkness left her unable to focus on anything around her. Her legs were bound together and her arms at her sides. She lifted her right hand as far as it would go, reaching for anything that would help her figure out where she was. Her fingertips touched the sheet of plywood that was above her face.

"Oh, my God. No, no, no!" Reagan screamed. She pushed her arms out to the sides . . . more wood. She reached above her head . . . more wood.

"Help me! Someone help me!" she called out.

No noise. No response. Reagan sobbed in the blackness of her wooden box. Breath after breath, she tried to fill her lungs with air. No matter how hard she tried, she could not take in enough oxygen to stop the claustrophobia.

"Jackson, help me!"

Jackson jumped up off the couch, waking from the torturous nightmare. Sweat poured down his face and soaked his shirt. His stomach ached and turned. He sprinted to the bathroom, hoping to make it before expelling the contents of his stomach, however little it was. After he flushed the toilet, Jackson stepped over to the sink. He stared at his face in the mirror, hardly recognizing the man looking back at him. He turned the knob marked with blue, cupped his hands together, and filled them with water. Over and over, he splashed his face, until he started to feel better. He clutched the gray hand towel hanging next to the sink and used it to dab his face.

When he finished, he stood in front of the vanity and stared at his reflection until his bloodshot eyes filled with tears. His shoulders shook from the weeping that overpowered him. Jackson's shaky knees buckled, and he collapsed to the floor. The cabinet door supported his vanquished body. He didn't know what to do. He didn't know where she was. But the thought that sickened him the most . . . he didn't know if she was even alive.

CHAPTER 17

The small hand of the clock had turned a full three hundred and sixty degrees since Jackson's collapse in the bathroom. He hadn't heard from Officer Baker in hours, and the agony of silence was eating at him. He looked at his watch again, the eighth time since he'd woken up from the horrifying dream. It now said 4:39. The fact that it had been twenty-four hours since she disappeared was not helping his nausea.

Jackson paced yet again. He was shocked at how many steps one person could take within the walls of one small apartment. Dying of thirst, he took a bottle of water out of the fridge and sat down in Reagan's painting chair. He tipped his head back, chugging nearly half the bottle before lowering it back down. The canvas she had started the day before remained on the easel. Jackson looked at it again, wondering what she was getting ready to paint. The only trace he had was the streak of sky blue she had brushed across the top of the canvas.

He gazed at the gorgeous hue, and his imagination began to fill in the rest of the picture. He closed his eyes. A field appeared. Flowers stretched as far as the eye could see. Purple irises, yellow daylilies, orange marigolds, and pink pansies decorated the green grass that lay below them. In the distance, old maples, walnuts, and oak trees reached for the blue sky that she had started. A stream snaked its way along the left side of the field. One doe and her fawn stood at the edge of the water, enjoying the opportunity to get a drink.

Jackson opened his eyes.

"The deer," he said to himself. "Thank you, Reagan."

His legs suddenly filled with energy that he hadn't felt all day. He ran out to his car, fired up the engine, and peeled out into the middle of the street as he pulled a quick U-turn. First gear, second gear, third gear. Jackson tried to get to his house as fast as he could, without hitting anyone. His tires screeched when he slammed on his brakes in the cul-de-sac.

David had the front door open before his son had even made it up the sidewalk. "Jackson, what's wrong?"

"What's Patrick's phone number?" Jackson demanded.

"Patrick? Patrick Tanner?"

"Yes, dad. The only Patrick we know. I need his number, now."

"Okay, why?" David questioned. He held his phone up and opened his contacts. "Why?" he asked again.

"'Cause he can help me find her," Jackson answered.

David glanced up at him with concerned eyes. "Jackson, son, please lay down and get some rest."

"I don't need rest, dad! I need to find her. Give me his number. Please!"

"I'm getting it. I'm getting it. But will you please tell me why?" David handed his phone over to his son.

"One day, last fall, we were workin' at that new donut shop, remember?" Jackson asked.

"Yes," his father answered.

"We were on our lunch break, eatin' sandwiches on the tailgate. Patrick and Henry were standing next to the truck, yackin' about hunting. Goin' on and on about the deer they had killed and mounted on the wall."

"Okay," David said.

"Anyway, I thought it was strange, 'cause Henry never talks about anything. But he wouldn't shut up about this cabin or something that he has outside of town. It's in the middle of nowhere, on a big piece of land he has. That's where he goes during hunting season. Patrick, of course, asked if he could hunt there." Jackson paused, examining the blank look on his dad's face. "Dad, Patrick knows where it is, and I *guarantee* that's where she's at. That's why I need to call him." Jackson looked at his dad's phone and hit send on Patrick's number.

"Hello?" Patrick answered.

"Patrick, this is Jackson from work. Hey, man. I need to ask you something and you need to keep it between us. It's super important, okay?"

"All right, man. What's up?"

"Where is Henry's hunting cabin? The one that you used a couple of times," Jackson said.

"It's like eight miles north of town," Patrick said.

"I gotta know exactly where it is. Please."

"Okay. Take sixty-three 'til you get to Miller Road, turn left, and it's, like, four miles down. You can't miss it. There ain't much there, except a creepy driveway that leads into the woods. Look for the pole by the drive. The one with the deer sign on it," Patrick finished.

"Thank you so much. Thank you," Jackson said.

"You're welcome. Is everything all right?"

"Yes, just please keep this between us," Jackson instructed again.

"Will do. No problem," Patrick replied.

"Appreciate it. See ya."

Jackson hung up the phone and immediately walked down the hallway and into his father's bedroom. He opened the gun cabinet and reached for the .30-30. One by one, he loaded the firearm.

David looked at the gun, then at his son.

"What are you doing, Jackson? You need to call the police," David said.

"Nope. No way. I've tried talkin' to them. I told them who it was, and they didn't believe me. He's just an unfortunate dude, at home with a cold," Jackson said, mocking the police.

His father stood there, staring at his son's pale skin and dark eyes. "Jackson . . ."

"Dad, either come with me or get out of my way. I'm going, whether you like it or not."

David nodded, taking in his son's words. He reached into the cabinet and removed the shotgun and box of shells.

"I'm driving," he told Jackson.

The men marched into the garage and climbed into David's pickup. David started the truck and backed out of the garage and onto the street.

"Nice parking job," he told his son, looking at the black sports car, sitting crooked in front of the house.

"Sorry, I wasn't really . . ." Jackson started.

"It's all right. Don't worry about it. So, which way am I goin'?"

"Head up sixty-three until you get to Miller Road, then turn left," Jackson instructed him.

"Okay."

David drove without another word spoken, while they left Newbrook and headed north. Jackson gazed out the window at the empty, unplanted fields. The feeling he had inside was indescribable. He didn't know if he felt more excited to find her or more worried about what he might find. The eight miles they had to travel to reach their turn were the longest miles he could remember in his life. A small part of him wanted to take his father's advice and call the officer who had been working so hard to help him out. But, deep down inside, he wanted to be the one to find her. He wanted to be the one to confront the asshole who took away the perfect angel in his life.

David slowed down as he approached Miller Road. The

humming sound of the tires on the pavement faded away, drawing Jackson's gaze from outside the window. David turned the truck onto the stone and crawled forward. The old, gravel road had seen better days. It was probably for the best that they had taken the truck, as the neglected ruts and potholes could have swallowed the car. Jackson gripped the gun with trembling hands.

"How far is it?" his father asked him.

"He said about four miles. Look for a pole by the road that has a deer sign on it," Jackson told him.

David nodded. They approached with caution, trying not to make too much noise or stir up the dust. The sun had lowered just enough in the sky to allow it to beam into their eyes. Patrick was right; it was in the middle of nowhere. Other than a few farmhouses and silos in the distance, there was no sign of civilization.

Ahead on the right, a large patch of woods stood out amongst the empty fields. Jackson and his father looked at each other, knowing they had made it. A tall wooden pole stood next to the overgrown path that led into the trees. The deer sign had almost rusted through.

"You ready?" David asked Jackson.

"Yes," he replied.

The tires rolled onto the dirt tracks, which were divided by a strip of tall grass. The truck itself squeezed between the trees lining the trail on either side. Branches scratched the windows and paint, making a horrible shrieking sound. At least two football field lengths had passed, when the small cabin finally appeared ahead.

Jackson's heart raced, his stomach cramped, and his knee bounced out of control. He searched around for any sign of Henry or his truck, but there was nothing there. Trash and scrap metal were piled up amongst the trees that surrounded the shelter. Rusty old cars, junk refrigerators, and barrels stood in a row along one side. David parked the truck and shut it off. "Look at all the crap," David said. "What's he doing with all this . . . this trash?" he asked, as he loaded the shotgun.

"Who knows, dad? He's got a screw loose," Jackson replied.

"All right, let's go."

They climbed out of the truck, taking care not to slam the doors shut. Jackson held the .30-30 up high, prepared for anything to come their way. After one lap around the house, it appeared abandoned. If one didn't know any better, they would assume that the shack hadn't had visitors in many decades. Jackson nodded toward the door, and David subtly acknowledged it.

Stair by creaky stair, their feet climbed onto the porch. David reached for the door and looked at Jackson, as if to ask him if he was ready. Jackson held his gun up and waited for the door to swing open. His father turned the knob and pushed the door in. Jackson entered slowly; the gun aimed to fire. David followed behind him with the shotgun. They scanned each room with care, looking at every wall and every bit of floor, for anything that would work to hide a human being. Jackson opened a closet, then another. David looked in the cabinets. The men looked at each other in confusion.

"We're missing something," Jackson whispered.

He stood in the living room and turned in place, searching for anything that stood out. Then his eyes focused on something he hadn't noticed before – a hutch, stretching from the floor to the ceiling. Its shelves contained no more than the layer of dust that had settled there over the years. Beneath the base was an area rug that looked particularly out of place. The entire setup was like nothing you would expect to find in a cabin meant for hunting.

Jackson stepped over to the hutch, while his father kept an eye out for Henry. He leaned the gun against the wall and attempted to look in the crack between the giant cabinet and the wall. There wasn't enough room to see. He grasped the end of the hutch in his hands and slid it sideways, the rug making it easier than expected. A padlocked door was revealed on the hidden wall.

"Oh, my God. Reagan! Reagan!" he called out.

"Hold on, I'll get the cutters," David said, running out to his truck.

He dug through his toolbox and returned shortly, with a pair of bolt-cutters. David snipped the lock on the door and Jackson pulled it open. They could immediately smell musty air from the dark room below. Jackson looked at his father with fear in his eyes. The men held up their guns and stepped into the blackness.

Each board felt as if it could fall beneath Jackson's feet. His pounding heart seemed loud enough to be heard by his father behind him. As his eyes adjusted to the dim light in the room, he was finally able to look around the dusty space. About five feet past the last wooden stair, the room turned to the left. David looked to the right, but only one broken chair lay in the middle of the floor. Jackson continued forward, nearing the corner with caution. With the firearm leading the way, he turned left. And there she was.

"Reagan," he called, rushing to her side. "Dad, she's over here." Jackson knelt beside her. "Reagan," he wept.

He couldn't bear to see her this way. She hadn't moved since the blow to her left cheek, which had left her with a bloody face and a black, swollen eye. Her hair fell in dirty clumps onto the floor. The flannel, pajama pants she had put on the day before were gray from the dust that had soiled them.

He and his father exchanged looks, both fearing the same thing. David lowered his hand down to her neck and pressed his index and middle finger on her jugular.

"She's alive."

Jackson let out a sigh of relief at the sound of his dad's words.

"But we need to get her out of here. I'm calling the police now," David said.

"Okay," Jackson replied.

David stood up and reached for his phone. Jackson took out his knife and cut the restraints from her wrists and ankles. He slung the gun over his back, then scooped her up into his arms and started to stand.

"Yes, my son and I need help. We've found the girl that was taken yesterday. Her name's Reagan Nichols," David said, standing in the light, beaming down from upstairs. "We're in some cabin about . . ."

David's voice stopped, the deafening blast from a rifle echoing through the room. The fired bullet pierced the body of Jackson's father. David dropped to the floor at the base of the steps.

Jackson stood, vulnerable, holding Reagan's unconscious body in his arms, with his weapon hanging behind him. A pair of filthy boots started down the stairs. Jackson took a step back and looked down at his father. David's blood had begun to soak his shirt, the phone still in his hand. Henry stepped onto the concrete floor, reached for the phone, and ended the call. He pointed the gun at Jackson, a grin forming on his grimy face.

"I always wondered what it would be like to shoot my boss," he said.

Jackson took a step back for every step that Henry took closer to him. Eventually, his back hit the wall. He looked at Reagan's bloody face, still unconscious, then he lifted his eyes to Henry. The anger he had bottled up was conveyed through his glare.

"What's wrong, Jackson? Daddy can't wipe your ass?"

"You better pray he's still alive," Jackson threatened.

"I better pray, huh? It's kinda funny when you're angry, pretty boy. I've dreamed of this day," Henry said. "Day in and day out, I watch your spoiled ass march into work like you own the place. Oh, that's right, daddy owns the place."

"He did you a favor," Jackson reminded him.

"Oh, give me a break. He hasn't given me shit. You guys could care less if I even exist."

"Then why did you stay? If it was that bad, why did you stick around?"

"'Cause I knew it would be the perfect opportunity to get back at the type of people that have treated me like dirt my entire life. I've just been biding my time," Henry said.

Jackson shifted his weight. Reagan's body was starting to get heavy in his already weakened arms.

"How about you put her back down where she belongs?" Henry suggested.

"The hell with you," Jackson said.

Henry stared back at him, with a blank, soulless expression. Then he smiled again. He seemed amused by his thoughts.

"She's very pretty, isn't she? A sexy woman. Don't think I haven't noticed it. Her curves. Her lips. Her hair – so soft between my fingers," Henry said. Jackson's blood boiled from the horrific words. "How's it make you feel inside, to know that she's been mine for hours? There was nothing you could do about it. You have no idea what I've done with her. You'll never know. No matter what you do, for whatever life I allow you to live, you'll never forget that, will you? Let that thought burn your insides, Jackson. It will eat you alive. And she'll be mine forever."

Jackson's arms were numb, shaking from the stress of mass and gravity. His adrenaline was the only thing giving him the strength to fight through it. He remained still, unwavering, and disciplined.

"I'm gonna tell you one more time . . . put her down," Henry demanded.

Jackson returned the evil grin that Henry had been delivering.

"Over my dead body," Jackson said.

"My pleasure." Henry started to lift the gun in his hands, when yet another boom echoed off the concrete walls.

Henry's body collapsed in the dirt.

Jackson looked at his father. David was propped up on his

side, shotgun still in hand, and aimed steadily at his target. The blast had entered Henry's back and, with one final gasp, his face rested on the floor.

"Dad!" Jackson screamed.

"His gun. Get his gun," David moaned, struggling to form words.

Jackson pulled the weapon away from the body with his foot, then shuffled over to his father. He gently laid Reagan down and leaned over David's body.

"Dad," he said, wiping the tears from his face.

"I'm okay," David said. "It doesn't even hurt."

Jackson sniffed and let out a laugh. "You really are the most stubborn person I know."

David smiled back at him. "Listen," his father told him.

Jackson lifted his head and listened to the beautiful sirens. He never knew he'd be so happy to hear them.

CHAPTER 18

Police officers stormed into the cabin, guns drawn.

"Down here!" Jackson screamed. "Help us!"

He crouched on the floor, one hand on his father and the other on Reagan. The cops stormed down the steps, Officer Baker leading the way. They came across Jackson and his loved ones at the bottom.

"They need an ambulance," Jackson said, his hands covered in his father's blood.

Officer Baker pushed the button on her radio. "Roll a second ambo to forty-four fifty, West Miller Road. I repeat, we need a second ambulance at forty-four fifty, West Miller Road." She glanced at the dead man lying across the room, and walked over to verify his status. She then knelt next to Jackson, examining the victims. "Jackson, I'm . . ." she began.

"It's okay. I should have called you sooner. I was just so angry, I wasn't thinking."

"No worries. Let's focus on them now. Is this your dad?" she asked.

"Yes, his name's David," Jackson answered.

"David, this is Officer Baker. Can you hear me?" He nodded

in return. "Good. I need you to hang in there, okay? The paramedics will be down in a minute to get you to the hospital."

"Take . . ." he began, struggling to stay awake. "Take Reagan first."

"Reagan is stable right now. We need to take you first, David."

The EMTs from the first ambulance arrived and had David ready to go in no time. They handed Jackson the keys from his father's hip, then he embraced his dad one more time before they carried him out. Reagan's ambulance showed up shortly after. The paramedics lifted her onto the stretcher.

"Is she gonna be okay?" Jackson asked.

"She doesn't appear to have any serious injuries. Looks like a pretty ugly bump to the head. We need to get her checked out, though," the paramedic informed him.

"Okay," he replied. He leaned over Reagan's body and tried to hug her the best he could. "I'll see you in a little bit, baby," he said.

Jackson kissed her, then backed up and out of their way.

"Jackson, I need a few minutes of your time, to ask you some questions, before you head to the hospital," Officer Baker said.

"All right."

"Start with how you got here," she said.

"A guy I work with, Patrick; he's been here to hunt before. Henry told him where it was. I called him earlier and asked him how to get here. Dad and I grabbed the guns and drove out, hoping we'd find her," he answered.

"And Henry was here when you got here?" she asked.

"No. We didn't see him anywhere. We looked around outside and walked through all the rooms. He wasn't anywhere. It took us a minute to find the door. He had that hutch slid in front of it. When we got down here, Reagan was on the floor by the shelves. Looked like she had been there for a while. Her wrists and ankles were tied up. She . . ." he hesitated. "She had blood on her face."

"It's all right," she comforted him. "Take your time."

He wiped his nose, then continued. "That's when I cut her ties and picked her up, and dad called 9-1-1. He was on the phone when that psycho shot him from the top of the steps."

"Yes, the operator reported the gunshot on the call. Go ahead."

"Henry came downstairs and hung up the call. I was still holding Reagan and he had the gun pointed at me. He kept telling me to put her down and I refused," he said.

"Then what?"

"He acted like he was gonna shoot me. Then dad saved us," Jackson told her. "He saved our lives."

"He shot Henry?" she clarified.

"Yeah. Henry assumed he was dead, I guess. He didn't even see it comin'."

She finished taking notes, then smiled at Jackson. "That's all I need right now, thank you," she told him. He nodded in return. "I hope they're okay. If you need anything at all, call me," she said.

"Thank you."

"Get out of here," she told him, nodding toward the steps.

Jackson didn't think twice about her advice. He took off up the steps, using every other stair. The sun had dropped even farther in the sky, now hovering over the horizon, leaving an orange glow in the west. Blue and red lights lit up the trees, as several police cars were still parked in front of the house. Jackson climbed into the driver's seat of his father's truck and left through the scratching trees.

At the hospital, Jackson pulled the truck into the first spot he could find, then sprinted toward the emergency room doors. He burst into the lobby, gasping for air. The woman behind the front counter looked at him with concern, as he attempted to catch his breath.

"Two people . . ." he started, taking another deep breath. "Two people were just brought in here. One was a woman. Reagan Nichols. The other was a man named David Holloway, with a gunshot wound. Is there any way I can see them?"

"The gentleman went into surgery. It's gonna be a little while before you can see him," the woman said. She studied the computer screen for a moment. "Reagan is still being examined. Tell you what, if you want to have a seat, I will let you know as soon as you can get back to see her. Okay?"

"Thank you so much," he replied. "And my father, David?"

"I'm unsure at this point when that will be. When they finish the surgery, he'll go to recovery. We can certainly notify you when he can have visitors."

"Okay. Thank you."

Jackson walked over to the nearest chair and took a seat. A red-headed woman was sitting with a little girl, on a bench seat across from him. The girl, no more than seven, stared at Jackson with fear in her eyes. She grabbed the woman's arm and whispered something in her ear.

"I don't know, honey. Don't stare," she told the girl.

Jackson glanced down at himself. The shirt that he had now been wearing since the day prior was stained with the blood of the two most important people in his life. His jeans were dirty and speckled with maroon. He flipped his hands over, the palms still red. It was obvious to him why the girl was frightened. He looked like the victim in a horror movie. Jackson looked at the girl and smiled.

"I'm okay," he reassured her.

"What happened?" the girl asked reluctantly. Her mother laid her hand on the girl's back and apologized to Jackson.

"It's all right," he reassured the woman. "Well, a couple people in my family were hurt."

"Are they okay?" the girl asked.

"Yes. They're gonna be okay now," he replied. The little girl smiled. "I probably oughta go change, though, huh?"

"Good luck to you. I hope they're okay," the woman told him.

"Thank you," he replied. Jackson stood up and walked back to the counter. "Uh, I'm gonna go home and clean up a little bit, but I'll be right back."

"Okay," the woman replied, smiling at him.

Jackson walked back outside and looked at his watch. It was almost dark out now. He walked in the glow of the light poles, back toward the truck. It suddenly dawned on him that no one knew what had happened yet. He climbed inside, plugged in his phone, and called Reagan's parents.

"Hello?" Barbara answered.

"Mrs. Nichols, it's Jackson. I wanted to let you know that we found Reagan."

Barbara started sobbing on the other end. "Is she okay?" she finally asked.

"Yes, she's okay. She's at the hospital. They won't let me back yet, though."

"Oh, thank God. Thank you so much," she told him. "Tim! Tim, they found her. She's at the hospital."

"Oh, my God. Praise Jesus," Tim said in the background.

"Jackson, you're an angel," Barbara told him.

"I'm sorry it took me so long," Jackson told her.

"Honey, don't you say that. You're a savior. We'll be there as soon as we can, okay?" she told him.

"Okay. She's at Newbrook Baptist. I'm running home real quick to change, but I'll be right back."

"Okay, sweetie. Thank you so much. You'll never know how much this means to us."

"Anything I can do, you tell me."

"Okay, hon. Make sure you take care of yourself, too. All right?" Barbara reminded him.

"I will."

"We'll see you shortly," she finished.

Jackson hung up and immediately called Jen, then Donna. By the time he had filled them in, he had already walked in the house and was picking out new clothes to put on. He set the phone down when he was done, and turned the shower on. Jackson closed his eyes and stood in the hot water, letting the warmth bring life back to his body. The water, while clear when it landed on his skin, ran pink off the end of his fingertips. After almost ten minutes in the shower, he donned fresh clothes, feeling completely renewed. When he left, he took his car, still parked crooked in front of the house.

On the way back to the hospital, he decided he should call his brother, to let him know what had happened. He had a lot of explaining to do, as Dallas was still unaware that anything had occurred at all.

"Hello?" Dallas answered.

"Hey, what's up?" Jackson asked.

"Not much. Just dreading finals coming up. What's goin' on?" Dallas chuckled for a second. "I don't think you've ever called on a Wednesday night before."

"Actually, I need to tell you something. It's kind of a long story."

"Okay . . ." Dallas said.

"Well, yesterday, one of the men at work took Reagan," Jackson began.

"Took her?" Dallas verified.

"Yeah. Took her right from her house. Sorry I haven't called before. It's been a crazy day," he said.

"Are you serious right now?"

"I wish I wasn't."

"Who the hell kidnaps a person?" Dallas asked in frustration.

"A whack job, that's who!" Jackson exclaimed. "Anyway, it's over now."

"What happened?"

"Well, I had a pretty good idea where she was, so dad and I went to get her. Then Henry showed up and shot dad . . ."

"What? Dad got shot?" Dallas screamed.

"Yes. He's in surgery. I'm on my way back to the hospital now," Jackson said.

"Oh, my God. Is he gonna be all right?"

"I think so. I won't know much 'til they tell me something."

"Okay, I'm comin'. I'll be there," Dallas told him.

"All right, I'll be at the hospital," Jackson told him.

"Baptist?"

"Yeah. I don't know where he'll be when you get here, so just call me when you get close."

"Okay. Is Reagan okay?" Dallas asked.

"She should be. She's got a gash on her head. They're checkin' her out. She was knocked out pretty bad."

"Aww, I'm sorry, man. That's awful."

"I know. It's killing me," Jackson replied.

"Wait, what happened to that guy, the one who shot him?" Dallas asked.

"I'm glad you asked," Jackson said. "After he shot dad, he turned the gun on me and Reagan. Then dad blasted him in the back."

"He's dead?"

"He's done, man."

"Way to go, dad!" Dallas yelled.

"He saved the day. I'd be dead if it wasn't for him," Jackson said.

"That's so crazy."

"All right, I'm almost back. I'm gonna get off here."

"Okay, I'll head over in a minute and call you when I get to town," Dallas said.

"Okay, see you in a little bit." Jackson hung up the phone as he put the car in park.

He strolled back into the ER, almost unrecognizable

compared to how he had looked the first time. The same woman sat at the counter.

"May I help you?" she asked.

"Yeah, I was hoping to check on Reagan Nichols and David Holloway," he said.

"Oh, yes. Let's see," she said as she referenced the computer. "David is out of surgery and in recovery."

"Good, good," he said.

"And it looks like Reagan is in room two forty if you would like to go see her."

"Yes! Thank you." He turned to walk away then doubled back. "Wait, how will I know when I can see my dad?"

"If you'd like to give me your number, I'll make a note in here for them to call you when he's ready," she told him.

"Yeah, that'll work," he replied. "Thank you."

She jotted down his phone number, trying to keep up with him as he uttered the digits in a hurry. He thanked her one last time, then did his best speed walk down the hall, until he found the right sign. It directed him to the group of room numbers he needed.

Jackson walked through the double doors, entering a giant room. The lights were all dim, except over the nurse's station in the middle. Individual rooms lined the perimeter. He started to the left, reading the number on each sign. Two thirty-seven, two thirty-eight, two thirty-nine . . . and at last, two forty. He passed through the open doorway.

Reagan was covered up and slightly elevated on the bed in the middle of the room. A single light on the wall and the monitor that displayed her vitals were all that allowed him to see. After all the rushing that he'd done to get there, he now had the impulse to slow down. As painful as it was, he stood at the foot of the bed for a moment, taking in the sight before him. Her feet, covered in the hospital-issued socks, stuck out of the end of the covers. Layers of thin, white blankets covered her body, which had been dressed in a gown. They had pulled her hair back and bandaged the lacerations on her face. There were two wounds; one on the left where he had struck her, and one on the right where her face had hit the floor. Dark bruises circled her left eye.

He pulled a chair up next to her and held her hand.

"Reagan," he whispered. A tear rolled down his right cheek. He wiped his face and spoke again. "Reagan."

Her face twitched a little, as she started to respond to his voice. She opened her eyes slowly and looked at the IV to her left. Jackson squeezed her hand a little and she turned her head toward him.

"Jackson," she said.

He kissed her hand. "Yeah, baby."

"You found me," she whispered.

He nodded, struggling to form words. "We did. Dad helped me."

"Thank you. Tell him I said thank you."

"I will," Jackson promised.

"What happened? I just remember him hitting me," Reagan said.

"I'll have to explain it later. I want you to rest right now."

"Where is he?" she asked. Her gaze was troubled.

"You don't have to worry about him anymore," he told her.

She closed her eyes at the sound of his statement. "Do mom and dad know?"

"I called 'em. They're on their way."

"They'll be devastated when they see me like this."

"Yeah, it's pretty hard," he replied.

"I'll be okay, honey," she comforted him. "Work. What about work?" she asked.

"They know. Jen knows, too. I'm sure they'll be here in a little bit. And Dallas is comin'."

"Aww, he doesn't need to do that," she replied.

"Well . . ." Jackson began. He tried to hide his expression, but was unsuccessful.

"What? What's wrong?"

"Dallas *is* coming to see you, but he's also coming to see dad."

"Your dad? What happened?" she asked, trying to sit up.

"Shhh," he said, hoping to keep her calm. "It's okay."

"What happened to your dad?" she repeated.

"He got hurt, that's all," he told her. She stared at him, waiting on him to finish. "All right, he might have got shot. But he's gonna be okay," he added, before she could react. "He's here, too."

"You need to go see him. I'm fine. Please, go see him," she insisted.

"I can't yet. They're gonna call me when he's out of recovery. Plus, I'm hoping you'll have some other visitors before I leave to go find him," he said.

"Like us," Jen said from the doorway. Donna stood behind her, already in tears.

Reagan looked at her friend and smiled. "Hey, girl," she said.

Jen looked at Reagan with a frown. "Lord, honey. Are you okay? Sorry, I know that's an obvious question, but are you?"

Reagan chuckled. "Yeah. Other than a headache, I feel pretty good." She looked at Donna, who stood sobbing next to Jen. "It's okay. Come here," Reagan said, waving her over.

Donna leaned down and hugged her. "Oh, I was so worried about you."

"I know, but it's okay now," Reagan said, as she patted Donna's back.

Donna stood up and dabbed her eyes. "Look at you, trying to make me feel better. I should be makin' you feel better."

"You are, just by being here," Reagan told her.

Jackson's phone started vibrating. "Hello?" he answered.

"Hi. My name's Carey. I'm your dad's nurse. I wanted to let you know that he's been moved out of recovery into a room."

Jackson exchanged looks with the girls in the room. They must have all been wondering the same thing. He stood up and walked out to find the voice he had heard outside the door. The nurse at the station still had the phone to her ear.

"Great, which room? I'll go see him," Jackson said to her, with the phone still in hand and a smile on his face.

The nurse looked very confused. "He's right over here in two forty-three," she said.

"It's okay, they're both with me," he told her. Jackson looked back into the room. "I'll be right back, okay?"

"Okay, honey," Reagan said.

He walked to his dad's room. David was still asleep from the anesthesia. Jackson stepped over to his bedside and looked at the bandages on his dad's shoulder. He couldn't help but think how lucky his father was that it hadn't hit a little lower.

"Oh, dad. I can't believe I dragged you into this," Jackson said. "I'm sorry I didn't listen to you and call the police. If I'd just listened to you, you wouldn't be here right now. Look at me, always calling you stubborn. I need to look in the mirror."

A subtle knock on the door got Jackson's attention.

"Sorry to disturb you, sir. Ms. Nichols was wondering if she could see Mr. Holloway for a moment," the nurse told him.

Jackson smiled and shook his head. "Why am I not surprised? She can't sit still. I can help her if you'd like," he offered.

"Actually, we had something else in mind," the nurse said with a smile. She moved her gaze to the curtain blocking the other side of the room.

"Can we?" Jackson asked.

"We sure can," the nurse said.

"Yeah, that's great!" he exclaimed. "Sorry, that came out louder than I planned."

"That's all right. Well, we'll get her moved over then," she told him, before walking out.

Jackson's phone started vibrating again. He glanced at it, then answered. "Hey, Dallas."

"Hey, I'm almost there. Is dad doin' okay?"

"Yeah, he's out of recovery."

"What room do I need to go to?"

"Two forty-three," Jackson told him.

"All right, I'll see ya in a minute."

"Okay, we'll be here," he said.

Jackson stood outside the room with Jen and Donna, as the nurse moved Reagan into her new space. They all seemed a lot more relaxed, now that they knew she would be okay. Dallas united with their group in time to join Reagan in the room.

"Jen, Donna, this is my brother, Dallas," Jackson said. "Dallas, this is Jen and Donna," he directed toward them respectively.

"Nice to meet you," Dallas said.

Jen glanced at Reagan, silently communicating the "not bad" expression.

Reagan mouthed the words, "He's taken," in return, chuckling at her best friend's optimism, despite the situation.

Even though it was already past ten o'clock, none of them seemed remotely tired. After all they had been through, Jackson and Reagan were still wide awake. Donna offered to get them some food, and they didn't hesitate to take her up on it.

"I bet your parents will be here soon," Jackson said.

"That's good. I hope they're doin' okay. This is late for them," she said.

"I'll call them if they're not here soon, and check on them," he replied.

David turned his head after his son spoke. "Jackson?"

"Dad. I'm here. Dallas is here, too."

"Is Reagan okay?" his father asked immediately.

Jackson, who had sat between them, scooted out of the way to give his father the line of sight. "How about you ask her yourself?"

"Reagan. Look at you. You look like you're feeling okay," David told her.

"I feel great, actually. Thanks to you guys."

"That's good. That's really good," he replied. David looked around at all the people in the room and grinned.

Jackson studied his father's expression. "What?"

"Nothin'. I was just thinkin', there's gotta be a better place for us to have a party."

CHAPTER 19

After discussing the idea with his father, Jackson and Reagan decided that there was indeed a better place for all of them to spend time together. When Memorial Day weekend rolled around, and they had all recovered from the tragic incident, David helped organize his dream-come-true cookout. Tim and Barbara made the trip down to stay for the weekend. Dallas was there, having just finished his first year of college. And last but not least, Jen and Donna were invited, too.

The weather on the day of their get-together was predicted to be an impeccable seventy-nine degrees, with nothing but sunshine. David and his children sat outside on the patio for much of the morning, as the damp, cool air started to warm up in the sunshine. Reagan's parents had stayed with her at the apartment. They all got ready for the day, then headed across town to the Holloways'.

Reagan led the way through the front door. "Knock, knock. We made it," she called out through the house.

"Morning," Jackson replied from outside.

Barbara looked out onto the patio. "David, this is beautiful. You have such a lovely home," she told him.

"Thank you, I appreciate that," he replied.

"You all look so great. I'm so glad you're feeling better," Barbara added.

"Whew, me too," David said.

"We brought some cookies. And I made a salad," Barbara told him.

"Thanks. That sounds great," he said.

"Mom, just bring 'em in here," Reagan hollered from the kitchen.

"Oh, okay, dear."

Tim stepped out onto the patio and shook hands with the man who preceded him. "Great place," he told David.

"Thank you, sir. I'm glad you guys made it," David replied.

"Me too. We haven't had a weekend away in quite some time."

"Well, kick back and relax. I hope you like barbeque. I got some chicken and ribs marinating in the fridge," David told him.

"That sounds great. I'd really like to give you a hand, though. Let me know how I can help," Tim insisted.

"Will do. We'll fire up the grill here in a little bit," David replied.

Tim started up a conversation with Dallas, and Jackson got up and walked inside. Reagan and her mother were still in the kitchen, organizing some of the food for the cookout.

"Come sit down," Jackson told them. "You're workin' too hard."

"We're about done," Reagan told him. "Just wanted to get a head start."

"What time are Donna and Jen coming?" he asked her.

"Donna should be here soon. The only reason she wasn't here at sunrise is because she wanted to wait until I got here," Reagan replied with a laugh. "I just told her I was here, so I'm sure she's on her way. Um, Jen was gonna go to the store for a few hours, I think, then she'll be here."

Jackson looked out the front window. "I'm pretty sure Donna just pulled up, actually."

"Oh cool," Reagan said. She ran over to the door and opened it, waiting on her friend to walk up the sidewalk.

"Is my car in a good spot?" Donna asked her.

"Yeah, you're good. We all parked in the driveway, so you and Jen would have room," Reagan reassured her. "Come on in."

Donna stepped inside. "Here's some potato salad. Made it myself. It's my mother's favorite recipe," she announced with pride.

"Thanks, that sounds great. I love potato salad," Reagan said.

"Oh, me too," Barbara said.

"Can you believe how gorgeous it is outside?" Donna asked.

"I know, it's amazing," Reagan agreed. She found a place for the potato salad in the already full refrigerator. "You wanna go sit outside? We set up some extra chairs for everyone around the firepit."

"You don't have to ask me twice," Donna said.

The girls strolled out to the patio and sat together on the swing.

"Nice to see you again, Donna. Glad you could make it," David said. "We got pop and water in the blue cooler and beer in the red one. Help yourself," he announced to the guests.

"Thank you. I may wait a little longer before I get a beer," Donna replied.

The men carried on their conversation about the potential of the Reds baseball team that season. Naturally, it was going to be their year. Barbara and Donna admired each other's blouses, each dying to know where the other had gone shopping. Reagan smiled. She wasn't certain if it was the warm, spring air or the comfort of family and friends. But she knew at that moment that everything felt like it would be all right.

About an hour later, Jen called Reagan to let her know she was on her way.

"All right, see ya soon," Reagan told her, before hanging up.

"Well, I think this is a good time to fire up the grill," David said. He walked inside to get the chicken and ribs, then came back out and lit the burners. "That potato salad looks amazing," he said.

"Why, thank you, David," Donna said.

One by one, he placed the pieces of meat on the grates and closed the lid.

"Dad, where we workin' next week?" Jackson asked.

"First Street. Residential job. Nothin' too bad," David answered.

"All right, cool," Jackson said.

"How long have you owned your company?" Barbara asked.

"Let's see," David said, counting to himself. "About twenty-one years now," he replied.

"That's great. I bet that takes so much dedication and hard work," she said.

"You got that right." He opened the lid to check on the meat. "It's nice, of course, 'cause havin' your own company gives you control over a lot of things. And you're your own boss. But sometimes, keepin' up with the guys and having all the responsibility can be exhausting. One wrong move and it can be over just as fast as it started."

"That's true. I can't imagine," Barbara said.

The sound of Jen's car door slamming shut could be heard out front. Reagan stood up.

"I'm gonna go get her."

Jackson looked up at his dad for a second, then smiled at Reagan. She glanced at David, who quickly turned back around to face the grill. Then she looked back at Jackson and smiled in hesitation.

"I'll be right back," she told him, trying to read the expression on his face.

She walked through the house and opened the door. Jen's knuckles were still held high in preparation for knocking.

"Woah, good timing," Jen said.

Reagan laughed. "I heard you pull up. Come on, we're all hangin' out on the patio."

"Is Dallas here?" Jen whispered.

"Yes, but I told you he's taken," Reagan replied, grinning.

"That's okay. Just gives me somethin' to look at," Jen told her.

"You kill me," Reagan told her. "Okay, come on." She led the way, with Jen right behind her.

"Hey, there she is," David said. "Good to see ya."

"Likewise. Thank you so much for inviting me. And that smells awesome," Jen added.

"Thank you, dear. I hope it tastes awesome, too," he replied.

Reagan and Jen took seats near the firepit.

"Were you busy this morning?" Reagan asked her.

"Not really. People had better things to do, I guess. They act like they have lives or something," Jen joked.

Jackson stood up. "I'll be right back," he told the group.

He gazed down at Reagan before he walked past her, another child-like grin on his face. His hand grazed her shoulder, then he opened the screen door and stepped inside.

"Ooo, what was that about?" Jen asked Reagan, nudging her in the arm.

"I have no idea. He's been all smiles today," Reagan said.

"Well, there's nothing wrong with that," Jen told her.

David flipped the meat again, marinating it as he went. Barbara and Donna continued to talk like they had known each other forever. Jackson came back to the screen door after a couple of minutes. He stood for a moment and looked out to the patio, full of family and friends. After a deep inhale and slow exhale, he walked back outside. Instead of getting back in his chair, though, he went over and stood next to his father at the grill. They exchanged a few quiets words, then Jackson turned around to face the group.

"Hey, uh, first I just wanna say thanks to everyone for comin'. You have no idea how happy it makes him to be able to do this," he said, pointing at his dad.

David shrugged his shoulders.

"Anyway, we wanted to have this opportunity to bring all of us together to enjoy this great food and, well, to enjoy life. But I personally wanna tell you how important you've all been to us – to me, to Reagan, and dad. It meant the world to us to have your support through all the bullshit that happened." He paused for a second before speaking again. "Well, I also needed you all here to celebrate something else . . . this amazing woman in front of me." Jackson gazed at her now. Her heart pounded in her chest. "Reagan, I don't know if I could ever come up with enough words or the right words to tell you how much I love you. I sure as hell can't picture life without you. For that day, that one terrible day, I couldn't talk to you, feel your head on my shoulder, watch you paint your pictures from heaven, or look at your beautiful face. I didn't know what to do. I couldn't eat. I paced more steps than most people probably take in a week."

Reagan wiped the tears from her face. The rest of the women were already doing the same.

"Listen to me," Jackson said. He walked over to her and crouched down at her feet. "I love you. I love you so much that I couldn't . . ." He faded off, bowing his head.

"Don't cry," she said, running her fingers through the hair on the back of his head. "I love you, too, Jackson."

He looked back up at her with red eyes and wet cheeks. "I want you to marry me," he blurted out. He opened his left hand, holding the ring in his sweaty palm.

Reagan took both of her hands to her face, stunned by what he was doing.

"I'm sorry," he said. "I'm not trying to pressure you or put you on the spot. I know we haven't been together long. We can wait a while, if . . ."

"Yes," she interrupted him. "Yes."

He wrapped her up in his arms and held her tight. It was silent for only a moment, until Barbara and Donna couldn't contain their excitement any longer.

"That was the sweetest thing," Barbara said.

"I know," Donna replied.

Reagan and Jackson smiled at each other, then looked at the women on the swing and busted up laughing. The two were holding each other like two teenage girls at a romantic comedy. Jen was in the process of blowing her nose. David's face was lit up, yet he still managed to babysit the grill with perfection. And even Dallas had an ear-to-ear smile, which consequently, Jen seemed to enjoy.

"This is for you," Jackson told her. He finally slid the ring onto Reagan's finger.

She gazed at the ring in awe. "It's so gorgeous. Jackson . . ."

"It was the best I could do," he replied.

"It's perfect," she said.

Jackson smiled. "And now . . . we spend our lives together."

CHAPTER 20

R eagan reached for a tissue and handed it to her daughter. Emma stared back at her mother, dabbing at her eyes with the tissue in hand.

"You all right?" Reagan asked her.

"Yeah, I just feel terrible," Emma told her. "I'm such a terrible daughter. You must hate me."

"No, honey. Don't say that. I could never hate you. I love you more than you know. You're my daughter, I'd do anything for you."

"That's my point. You're so loving and caring. Doesn't matter how horrible I've been, you never seem frustrated with me. How can you be so . . . nice?" Emma asked.

Reagan laughed. "Well, for starters, you're my daughter. Like I said, I love you."

"But I'm so horrible sometimes."

"No, I don't think you're horrible. I think you're a sixteen-year-old young woman, who's starting to grow up and figure out who she is. It's not an easy age," Reagan encouraged her.

"Thanks, mom." Emma twiddled her thumbs for a minute, as if holding back what she wanted to say.

"What's wrong?" Reagan asked.

"Nothing. I . . . I was wondering . . ." Emma hesitated.

"Are you wanting to ask me about what happened?"

"Yes. But we don't have to talk about it if you don't want to."

"It's all right, you can ask me," Reagan told her.

"I just wanted to know . . . did that guy . . . did he try to . . ." Emma trailed off.

"He never touched me. Not like that."

"Okay." Emma dabbed at her eyes again. "Okay, good." Reagan caressed her daughter's back, hoping to give her at least a little comfort.

"You had to be so scared," Emma continued.

"I was terrified, especially at first. Then I remember feeling angry. Maybe the angriest I've been in my life. To feel like someone could try to control me or steal my life away from me. It was infuriating," Reagan said. "But it's all okay now. I'm still here. I still have my life. I have you and I have your father. And I will always thank him for that. And your grandfather, too. For the risk they took to save my life. I will never forget that."

Emma nodded, then took her gaze away from her mother again. Reagan studied her expression, trying to figure out what her daughter was thinking but wouldn't say.

"Mom, you were right. When you said that Evan is arrogant and controlling, you were right. I hate that about him, but I love him, too. I don't know what I'm supposed to feel."

"What is your gut telling you?" Reagan asked.

"I don't know. I mean, I think I know, but I don't want to accept it," Emma answered. "I keep thinking, maybe if he grows up a little, some of that will go away."

"Ah, but you can't do that. No matter how much you think or hope that he will change, you can't expect him to. Evan is Evan, just like you are you. Listen to your gut, it's usually right," Reagan advised her. "If there is any doubt or bad feelings at all, well . . ."

"I know," Emma mumbled.

"And I'm sure you don't want to hear this from your mother,

'cause it's something that all mothers say, but you are so young. You have your whole life ahead of you. Think of all the amazing things you still get to see and do. You have two years of high school left. Time with friends. Dances. Football games to watch. And before you know it, you'll be graduating, and you can be so many things. You can pursue a life that you love." Reagan stopped for a moment, trying to find a way to get to the point. "Listen, Emma. If you and Evan are meant to be, then you will be. You will know. Just try to not miss all the fun things in the meantime, okay?"

"Okay, mom," Emma said. "I love you."

"I love you, too, honey." Reagan looked at her watch. "You better get ready. He'll probably be here soon."

"Yeah. You know what? I may go see a movie with Samantha. There's this lovey-dovey movie out that she's dying to see. I think I'll call her and see if she wants to go," Emma said.

"That sounds fun, but please don't change your plans because of anything I said," Reagan told her.

"I'm not. She actually asked me first and I feel bad 'cause I told her I was busy. Plus, he will understand, right?" Emma asked.

"That's right," Reagan agreed. "Hold on, I'll get you some money." She walked to her bedroom and opened her purse to get the wallet from inside. She carried it back out and handed Emma fifty bucks. "Here, this should be more than enough to get you into the movie, get snacks, whatever you want."

"Thanks, mom." Emma hugged her mother, then immediately called Samantha to ask if she was still up for a movie. After a couple of minutes, she hung up the phone. "She's so excited. I'm gonna go get my purse." Emma exclaimed.

She strolled to her room with a new spring in her step. Reagan smiled at Emma's excitement. It had been a while since her daughter had looked so eager to spend time with one of her friends. Emma walked back into the dining room and stood before her mother.

"How do I look?"

"You look great," Reagan told her. "Have fun."

"We will. What time do you want me home?" her daughter asked.

"Let's go with midnight," Reagan told her.

"Okay," Emma answered. She hugged her mom again. "Thank you," she said with sincerity.

"You're welcome, honey. Now go have fun," Reagan said.

"Okay, bye." Emma bolted out the door.

Reagan watched her daughter back out of the driveway, then she turned and walked into the backyard. She found Jackson crouched down next to the garden.

"Whatcha doin' out here?" she asked him.

He was on his knees, where the grass met the garden soil.

"Oh, pickin' these tomatoes. They're growing like crazy. What are we gonna do with all of 'em?"

"Guess you better start cannin'," she said. "Just kiddin'. I'm sure I can find a few people who would like some."

"Did Emma take off?" he asked.

"Yup. Just you and me. Got any ideas for supper?" she asked him.

"How about pizza and a movie," he suggested.

"That sounds great, actually," Reagan agreed.

"All right, I'll come in and get cleaned up," he said.

She called the family-owned pizza restaurant up the road and ordered their specialty pizza, minus the peppers and onions, of course. Jackson changed into his comfy clothes and curled up next to Reagan on the couch to wait on their dinner.

"So, what kind of movie are you in the mood for?" she asked him.

"Eh, it doesn't matter to me. But nothing too sad," he said.

"I agree," she said, checking out the choices.

"I heard you talkin' to Emma a little bit ago," Jackson said.

"Yeah, I thought it might be a good time for us to have a little heart-to-heart."

"Ooo," he responded with a grimace. "How was that?"

"I was a little surprised. It went pretty good," she told him. "A little ugly at first but, in the end, I think she heard what I was trying to tell her."

"And what was that?" he asked.

Reagan smiled at Jackson, then replied. "That she can be who she is, enjoy every moment she can, and to never let anyone try to take it away."

Dear reader,

We hope you enjoyed reading *Everything I'm Not.* Please take a moment to leave a review, even if it's a short one. Your opinion is important to us.

Discover more books by Sara Mullins at https://www.nextchapter.pub/authors/sara-mullins

Want to know when one of our books is free or discounted? Join the newsletter at http://eepurl.com/bqqB3H

Best regards,

Sara Mullins and the Next Chapter Team

ABOUT THE AUTHOR

Sara lives in southern Indiana with her husband and three children. She received a Bachelor of Science in Biology from Purdue University and enjoys spending time outdoors. When she's not camping or boating with her family, she loves expressing her creativity through writing, photography, and painting.

Made in the USA
Monee, IL
20 July 2021